Hellsong Series

Infidels: Cris

DUST

SHAUN O. MCCOY

SISYPHEAN PUBLISHING

Dust

Copyright 2017 © by Shaun McCoy

Editor-in-Chief: Gabrielle Olexa
Associate Editors: Kitty Garner, Andrew Anderson, Justin Williams, Meredith Oliver

Title art: Dusan Arsenic
Title Layout: Kirill Simin

A Sisyphean Publishing Book

Http://hellsongseries.com

ISBN-13: 978-0692856611 (Sisyphean Publishing)
ISBN-10: 0692856617

First Edition March 2017

Printed in the United States of America

0 9 8 7 6 5 4

PRAISE FOR SHAUN O. McCOY AND THE HELLSONG SERIES

"McCoy is a talented and bright young writer. Knight of Gehenna is a new kind of novel—a page turner in the truest sense—wrought from equal parts brawn and brain."
—*B. Butler, Author of Murder in Cairo*

"McCoy is a brilliant writer; insightful, intelligent, articulate, imaginative, and funny."
—*McKendree Long, Author of No Good Like it is*

"McCoy masterfully creates characters, scenarios and the Hell where they live. He writes with a passion, layering emotion on fantasy and science fiction, drawing in readers from beyond his genre."
—*Ginny Padgett, President of SCWW*

"Shaun is the real McCoy."
—*Laura Valtorte, Filmmaker, Author of Family Meal*

"McCoy again mixes freakishly paced action with deep emotion and a subtle plot. Soulfall blurs the lines between genres: one part Fantasy, one part Science Fiction, one part Literary Fiction—this sequel delivers."
—*Matt Michaelis, Author of Kids Summon*

"McCoy will certainly go to Hell for writing Soulfall . . . but it was probably worth it."
—*Justin Williams, Author of Blind Faith*

OTHER WORKS BY SHAUN O. McCOY

HELLSONG SERIES: ARTURIAN
Even Hell Has Knights
Knight of Gehenna
March Till Death
Book IV (2018)

HELLSONG SERIES: INFIDELS: CRIS
Affliction
Soulfall
Dust
Convalescence
Execution
Wasteland
Restoration

NOVELLAS
Electric Blues
Binary Jazz

This book is for Alison Reeves

ACKNOWLEDGEMENTS/FORWARD

This was not an easy book to write. Nor was it a book I'd intended to write as *Soulfall* had been originally plotted with a different arc.

Looking back on it now, though, this is the book I was *supposed* to write. Many thanks to Gabe for keeping me on track.

I should also thank Carson, my Brother-in-Law, since one of his insights on parenthood made it into this book.

Oh, also, if you're into **trigger warnings**, this is it. I'm not sure how you made it this far, but stop now! Go read something else.

From Neostoicism: Philosophia

Pain is no wound.
—Ares

Beware of that man who truly believes they do not lie, for they have deceived themselves first of all. It is his destiny to become a slave of the narrative he did not realize he himself created.
—Endymion

My son is going to kill me.

There Aiden crouches, his expressionless face half-illuminated in the violet haze, his eyes two perfectly black pits of soulless, murderous sadism.

He'd found me first.

I'm not sure how. El Cid and Q are certainly better trackers. Maybe Aiden was just closer. Maybe he just got lucky. Maybe Cid and Q have abandoned me.

Blue light crashes into the chamber, strobing in and out with the intensity of an old world lightning storm. Only there's no thunder, just the dull roar of the Erebus. It drowns out the purple light of Q's sword, revealing the entirety of my son's face. He is nothing if not patient

. . . and why not? What have the dead but time?

He approached me twice before. On both occasions I managed to raise Q's sword, and he drew back—either because he bought my bluff of violence or because he was just biding his time.

Is it a bluff, though? Can I bring myself to kill my own son? Am I strong enough to lift the blade a third time?

The infidels haven't abandoned me. I know they haven't. They're cruel sometimes. They make choices designed to cut their losses. They leave people behind. But they didn't here, because . . . because . . .

The blue light fades away.

My son stares at me from the purple-lined darkness.

"Do you dream?" I croak.

Speaking awakens the fire in my throat.

He doesn't answer.

In the old world, a man could die in relatively good spirits. Hell is not so made. As the body passes, the weight of its dying begins to rest on the soul—just as my dehydration bears down on me now.

I feel a burning building up inside me. Perhaps it's the burning of damnation.

Without any water in my body to fight the blaze, it rages unchecked.

My heart beats faster in my chest, pounding angrily against the dying of the blue light. Even my eyes feel dry, and the still air stings them. I would close them if not for my murderous son, crouching, waiting, brooding.

"Do you dream?" I croak again. "What do wights dream?"

The question is a trick. I'm trying to find out if he sleeps. If he closes his eyes, I'm going to crawl away— and I would have to crawl.

I don't know if my ankle is broken or just severely sprained. Either means death.

Do I even have the energy to try?

I stare at my son, fighting a losing battle with my delirium. Insanity swirls around me, just on the edges of my vision, crashing in upon my consciousness like the blue light, bringing with it soft dreams of peace and fire.

He still doesn't answer. The flames burn gently in my throat, in my body, in my mind. They lift me. I can feel the ground under my feet. I can walk toward the Erebus. Fire fills me so completely that only the black river can douse my soul.

No.

Not real.

I force my mind back into my body, back into the present where I lay half-propped up against the cave wall.

Clothes rustle as my son stands.

His soft footsteps reach my ears, just barely, over

the rush of the Erebus.

I want to grab Q's sword, but my arm will not obey my command. It twitches, like a branch popping in an intense fire.

I try to tell Aiden to stay away. My mouth opens, but nothing comes out. The air is like sand in my eyes, and my vision is so blurred that my approaching son is merely a shadow.

I feel him above me, and I wait for death.

His cold, dead fingers press into the skin around my mouth. I can do nothing to resist. Some foreign substance touches my lips, then my teeth and my tongue and my cheeks. Then the back of my mouth and my throat.

Water.

I swallow it like a man possessed. The fire in my body seems to make it steam, and for a moment, that steam is hotter than even my soul, but then the rush of the cool, cool liquid fights the inferno. Relief travels down, down, down into my belly where I feel the flowing waters quenching the fires of my damnation.

God it feels good.

Suddenly the water is gone, but the coolness remains. The beat of my heart slows. My breathing is rapid, but soon that too begins to calm. He's not here to kill me. My son is not going to kill me.

I'm starting to regain my faculties. I can see, I can think, I can focus.

But there's another sense I've forgotten, one which I would not have thought important. I can taste. And there's something in the back of my throat, brackish and rotting.

No.

I look to my son, crouching back in his corner.

"You can't!" I shout.

The taste is a new one, but slightly familiar. It reminds me of the corpsedust Hagar had poured down my throat in Maylay Beighlay . . . but it's somehow smoother, purer. Not corpsedust, but wightdust.

My son is smiling, blue light shining against his otherwise purple covered face. "You don't get to die, Father. Not without permission."

How much wightdust does my son produce? How much does it take to turn a man? Does the fact that I'm nearly dead change this? If he kills me now, will I become a wight straight away, or will I become a corpse first?

Patient, still unmoving, my son abides.

He's going to get a father, it looks like, one way or another. Can I blame him for wanting such a thing?

I have energy now. Perhaps I'm strong enough to kill him. Well, physically I might be. Mentally, though, after everything I did to keep him alive . . .

Does this quiet and brooding thing even count as my son? Maybe now is the time to make a break for it.

I'm still only a few feet from the Erebus. I can try dragging myself to the cliff—but even if I somehow survive a fall, with this ankle, I will surely perish in the wilds.

He speaks, "Are you in pain?"

"This isn't . . ." my voice breaks.

He holds up the canteen.

Jesus Christ. He's going to keep feeding me that. Slowly but surely, I'll turn. Everything I am, everything I've become, all my learning about Hell and its people, about its landscapes and its demons, all of that will be used against other human beings.

I look back toward the Erebus.

"Are you?" he asks.

I turn to him.

He cocks his head to one side. "Does it hurt you, when you think about killing Mother?"

I cannot so much as hear Myla's name without hearing her song picking up again.

Sometimes, I feel . . . like a motherless child.

The image of the dying workers in Maylay Beighlay assaults me. I'd killed them, virtual innocents, so I could get to Myla. Maybe Aiden doesn't have to fill me with wightdust. Hell, you can pretty much leave me on my own, and I destroy everything around me. Friends, enemies, it hasn't mattered.

And sometimes, I feel . . . like a motherless child.

I've got to be better than this.

"Nothing?" he asks.

"I had to kill her," I say, ignoring the fire in my throat. "Aiden, she was destroying you."

"She?" He comes to his feet. "*She* was destroying me?" He is angry, terribly angry, but unlike the voice of an emotional human child, the voice of this wight does not quaver. "Mother and Xyn did more for me than you. They raised me. They taught me to survive in Hell. You didn't do anything. You just killed them. You kept me on edge, in torture, for *weeks!*"

A long ways . . . from home.

Oh, son. I love you so much. "I had to."

"You had to torture me?" he asks. "I was in so much pain the infidels, the God damned infidels, wanted to mercy kill me. You killed the only people I ever —"

"Look, you think that now. But Myla and the Archdevil, they were poisoning you, someday you'll . . . you'll . . . "

Someday—but it isn't ever going to be like that, is it? Not now. I'd clung to hope. To the idea that things would get better for him. But he doesn't want to be saved. He thinks the devils are the ones who love him. Someday is gone now, he's a wight. There will be no someday. There will be no happy young man who will come to know and love his father. There will be no adolescent who, after a few years of growth, will understand how Myla wronged him. Who will understand that I rescued him. Who will understand why I did what I did.

. . . in the Heavenly land. Way up . . . in the heavenly land.

The inferno returns inside me, raging. Aiden better dose me fast or I'm liable to die right now.

I open my eyes. He's still there, crouching again in his corner. He's got a canteen ready, held between both hands. I bet he's got wightdust mixed in with it already. The brackish aftertaste of the last dose I received still lurks in the back of my flaming throat.

His head inclines a little, and I wonder if those black eyes are focused on me.

Then he speaks, "You hate God. Doesn't that mean you have to side with the devils?"

I look at the ceiling. After a moment, I push myself up so I'm resting against the stone wall. My swollen foot throbs from the motion.

"No. I hate them, too."

Aiden nods. "I don't think it's safe to pick fights with both sides."

"I bet you're fucking right."

I shouldn't curse at my son, but really, as he's already spiraled downward from problem child to monster, a few fucks are just a metaphorical spit in the bucket.

"I am," he says with the calm self-assurance of a

religious demagogue, "and the more of me you drink, the more you'll see that. I'm on your side, Cris. You're going to understand why. You'll see why the Devil wants people to resist. Why he wants people to be like you and fight Hell. I'm going to help you."

Help me? He's right about one thing. All this shit he's been saying about how I'm in the wrong, about how I shouldn't have killed Myla and the Archdevil, it's going to start making sense to me. Bit by bit, drop by drop, swallow by swallow, I'm going to start agreeing with him.

I crawl for the ledge.

"Stop!" Aiden cries.

My right ankle is useless, but I don't need it. Arm over arm, my left leg pumping, I head into the cave which opens to the Erebus. The river of darkness is a terrifying thing, a rush of evil pierced by stretches of snakelike lightning which worm their way through its dim clouds. I pause at the ledge, wind whipping at my hair, vertigo overcoming my senses. Those depths, they are infinite. How long can I fall before I hit one of those electric streamers? Would I be at peace for that long at least?

"Please." There are tears in Aiden's voice. "Don't leave me. Not again. You can't leave me again."

My heart breaks. I look down the ledge and watch the rush of the black, mistmade river.

"Don't leave me all alone," Aiden begs, inching

closer.

Something in his tone reminds me of the boy I'd known so long ago. The one who couldn't tie his shoes. I don't really want to die.

"Okay," I croak. "Okay. But only if you give me water. No wightdust."

He shakes his head. "Half portion."

I push forward, my torso now hanging over the abyss.

"Wait!" he yells.

I pause, inching back a little. "No wightdust."

"Okay, okay. And we'll save people?" Aiden asks tentatively.

Save people? The hell? Fuck if I understand what's going through his mind. "Of course. We'll save people."

I look back at him. He's pondering this now.

"Okay," he agrees.

He twists the cap off the canteen and pours its contents onto the ground.

Warily, I crawl away from the ledge.

Aiden wakes me, and I feel water running down my throat. This time it's pure. I can't pretend to understand what's going on. Maybe he's smarter than me. Maybe this is part of his long con. Maybe this is the Devil preventing me from taking that suicide option so he can still use me as a weapon.

After the water, Aiden hands me a chunk of some

raw dyitzu meat.

"I've taken your sword," he tells me. "You were asleep, but you need more than water if you're going to live."

I nod.

"It's right for you to stay alive and in pain, that's good," he says, his black eyes narrowed as if he's working something out. "But I love you, so I want to spare you. Whenever it hurts too much, if you want to take the wightdust, let me know."

I need to figure him out. He doesn't want me dead. He wants to hurt people, but he also wants to save them.

I bite down on the raw meat. The devil's blood fills my mouth as I chew.

"As soon as you can walk, we need to find Mom's body," Aiden says. "We can be a family again. Even if she's just a corpse."

I almost vomit up the water I just drank. "Are you fucking serious!" I shout.

A wave of blue fills our room, lighting up his face. He stands, his black eyes wide.

"No," he breathes, but he's not talking to me.

Then I hear something, someone, a call in the distance.

"You promised!" Aiden wails.

Footsteps are coming this way. They sound booted. Neb maybe?

Aiden darts away through the cavern's exit.

"Dammit!" I shout.

But it's too God damned late.

He's gone.

Myla's voice soars.

And sometimes, I feel . . .

It's a series of bootsteps, too many and too loud to be Q and Cid. Maybe they'd gotten help? It has been some time. Maybe they needed—

A single figure appears beyond the shadows where my son had fled. When he takes a step forward, I cannot hear the footfall. The dim lighting of the cave only illuminates my savior from the waist down. He's wearing old world leather hiking boots of some kind, with soft soles and metallic loops for the laces. His pants are dyitzu hide, dark in color, probably from some dye, but I suppose it's possible that the devil could have been that dark. At his belt is a sword. I can't quite see the hilt, but I can say almost for fucking sure it's an infidel weapon.

Oh thank God.

The fear races out of me and I let myself take in a deep, deep, deep breath. Then I let it go, and try to forget that my soul has been ruined. That my son is gone. That I have nothing left to live for.

"I'm glad you—" I begin.

A flash of blue light bursts into the room, illuminating the figure in full. The silver-hilted blade sheathed at his waist is Cid's. His shirt is made from the same dark colored hide as his pants, though it's been ripped open at the shoulder by the clawing hands of some devil. Blood stains cover his clothes, slick and reflective, seeming black in the sudden azure strobe. He's got what I think is a shotgun slung over his shoulder, and its strap is half filled with shells. At his side, in a policeman's holster, is a pistol of some kind. His face is pale, wan, and familiar. Eyes, unmistakably blue, are sunken behind dark circles. Cheekbones, both strong and somehow fine featured, jut out, matching the obtrusive handsomeness of his supermanesque cleft chin. His hair, midnight black, is interrupted by a thin streak of pure white where some horror must have touched his soul.

Keith.

His cancer men filter in around him, human hyenas who keep to the darkness. They crouch in the black alcoves of the room, their stubble-filled faces occasionally visible in the inconstant light of the Erebus. Amongst them I see Durgan, the marble-skinned wight from Maylay Beighlay. I knew it. I knew Keith had him.

I hear the far off call of a Fury, shouting its trainlike cry into the Erebus. Keith walks toward me, silent as death, slow as time, and kneels down beside me.

"Hello, Godslayer," he says softly as the hellacious blue lighting comes and goes, and comes and goes. His fingers reach out, touching my cheek in an almost caring gesture.

The laughter of his hyena men drowns out the distant call of the Fury.

Durgan approaches, standing over Keith's shoulder, his stonelike face and black on black eyes glistening in the shaky light.

The depth of my failure dawns on me.

I've been a terrible father. It's true, I did my best to recover, and I put together a good run at the end. I chased my bewighted son for three God damned years before killing a fucking Archdevil—but I just couldn't make things go right. Aiden, I couldn't make you love me. Those early years, they were my undoing. I gave you enough pain to justify your becoming a monster, then I gave you the means to become one. I'm just so fucking tired of being out of control. Of being not good enough. Of losing in the one place where a man can't have excuses.

I'm a failure as a father.

I roll over onto my stomach to get away from Keith's caressing hand. There is only one thing I can control. Again I crawl for the ledge.

Hell, have you a Fury for me, or will I die upon your cruel rocks as I tumble?

A cold hand, hard as stone, grabs my wounded ankle. Dear fucking God, that hurts. I bite deeply into my lip and try to propel myself forward with my elbows, but I can't.

"Oh, no, no, no," Keith says, laughing. "You don't get to die, Godslayer. Not for a long, long, time."

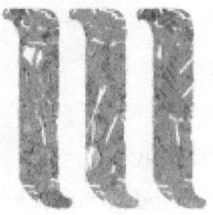

I reach up through the darkest depths and grab with my outstretched fingers a single silver strand of wakefulness. It cuts deeply into my palms as I pull myself, bit by bit, hand over hand, into consciousness.

The fire is there in my throat again.

I awake with a start in a dim room—my brain trapped in some deep fog and my arms struggling against the bonds which hold my beyond-numb hands behind my back—but I close my eyes as soon as I realize they're open. It's probably better if they don't know I'm awake. In that flash of vision I saw red faces around a smokeless fire. Tired faces. Terrified faces.

Did anyone notice me stir? My heart slows down as

I force myself to take even breaths. As the moments pass my mind clears, and gradually the sound of the men's whispered voices begins to reverberate in my brain.

"I see it when I close my eyes."

"Get the fuck over it, man."

"Look, I know you're feeling it too. We're all fucked up. This isn't the time to be tough."

"I don't need your God damned help, Alec."

Then sleep claws again at my mind. No, not sleep, unconsciousness. I don't dare let myself succumb to the blackness. For one, I'm afraid that if I slip down into that morass again, I might never return. And for another, I'm a prisoner. My only chance at survival is to understand and outwit my captors. A prisoner has to be the most dangerous kind of man if he is to survive. He must be an opportunist with a plan.

I've got the first box checked.

I can't count on rescue. I'd lain on the banks of the Erebus for far too long. Undoubtedly, Cid and Q had been forced to leave.

I really am alone, and there are so many questions I need answered. I'd known Keith and his hyenas intended to take me alive since Dendra, but what use could I possibly be to them?

And is my son here? I understand why he ran. He didn't know who was coming. But will he try to follow them? Would he view Keith as an ally or an enemy? I guess it would all depend on if he heard Durgan's voice or not. Durgan and Aiden had presumably spent some time together in Maylay Beighlay.

The temptation to open my eyes is driving me crazy, but I fight the urge. If my son is here, then I'll find out soon enough. Nothing will change in the next few minutes if I see him, except that the men around me will speak less freely.

"I don't want to go in there."

"It's where our home is."

"It's worse in there. Let's stay here. Let's never leave."

"Durgan will lead us through safely."

"Like he just did?"

"No. God no. I hope not like that. We've lost enough men already."

Cid had called them a cancer. A group of people who took the successful ideas the infidels had gathered and used them to pursue a vastly different agenda. Knowledge is a powerful tool, but there's nothing in human nature that demands it be used for good. I think her title for them is spot on. They truly are a cancer.

I had cancer in the old world, and I know a thing or two about the spirit of the affliction. People think cancer is death, but it is not death. Cancer is life. It is the abundance of life that leads to death. And these men, they form this cell, warped by some mutation away from its normal purpose. That cell then multiplies and spreads throughout the system, destroying all that the infidels had hoped to achieve.

For just a moment, I feel my own soul beneath my black pit of depression. There is a yawning chasm of emptiness where the purpose of my life used to lie.

There's nothing left for me to live for.

I bury that thought beneath the ample rubble of my previously shattered blocks of self-denial. Escape first, then face the existential emptiness which threatens to swallow your soul. You think such a denial would be hard, you know, but it's not. Humans were built this way. Built to bury their thoughts deep under the lies.

I have a task. I must learn my enemy—then destroy them from within. Motherfuckers, you can call me chemo.

I listen and learn, memorizing their names and their voices, peeking from time to time to attach a face to a name . . . then I drift back into sleep.

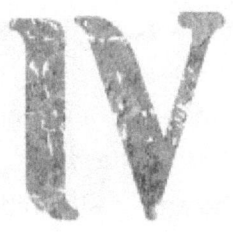

IV

I'm disturbed by their arguing. This time I awaken with more grace, and I'm almost positive no one noticed me.

"That is utter and total bullshit, Keith." That's Harris.

I'd learned his voice earlier, and I'm pretty sure I know which face that voice belongs to as well. He's a black man, but his voice is indistinguishable from a Midwestern Caucasian one. For whatever reason, he's the only one that will dare speak up to Keith.

"I'm saying it's a possibility." Keith's tone is unbothered by Harris' anger.

"You listening to this shit, Durgan?" Harris gives a nervous laugh. "You're thinking Godslayer over here is some two-bit untrained son-of-a-bitch?"

Wait a minute. That's me. *I'm* the Godslayer. Keith had called me that for some reason as I'd crawled toward the Erebus.

I keep my breathing even and make sure not to move.

There is a moment of silence. I imagine all the hyenas turning to stare at Durgan.

"I am indeed listening—to this . . . shit," Durgan answers as if dissecting the meaning of the colloquial curse.

There is more silence.

"He killed Xyn, man," Harris says. "He killed our *God*. I'm telling you, this motherfucker over here probably orders Ares and Endymion around."

Their God? Does he mean the Archdevil? That Archdevil was claiming to be *the* Devil, not a God—but in Hell, I suppose it amounts to the same thing.

"Gods ain't supposed to be dyin'." That's Clement.

I start coming up with some associations to help me remember their names. Clement is what Mason of Cid's group would be—if Mason were a total shithead with long blond hair. That being said, old Clement/evil-Mason here has a good point. I'm pretty sure one of the things a God is supposed to be is immortal.

There is some tension in the air. I guess Clement has stepped close to that line called blasphemy.

"Did you hear that?" Alec's harsh whisper cuts us

all short.

Alec's been quiet so far—so much so that I gave him and that Ryan fellow the nickname mute—but he spoke up for this.

I hear everyone's breathing.

"You didn't hear shit," Harris' whisper is equally harsh, but it is a whisper, so he must have given the threat some credence.

They wait for some time, their conversation on hold as they listen for enemies.

"You're fucking paranoid," Clement mutters.

"They're out there, man. I can hear 'em." Alec sounds completely unhinged.

I'd thought the Order would be more, well, in control of themselves.

"Yeah? What the hell is it you hear?"

"I don't know man, but it's out there."

"He might be hearing hellsong," Fin says.

"Jesus, Fin, you're so stupid," Harris answers. "We're too far from the Erebus."

"But you can still hear hellsong," Fin snaps back. "You can hear it anywhere. Stop acting like I'm stupid."

There's a sigh I believe came from Keith.

"Look, I know how you feel, Harris." Keith's voice is noticeably softer this time. "Xyn was my god too. What you have to appreciate is—"

"He was never your god," Clement breaks in, his hushed, southern voice shaking a little with the venom of his accusation. "You've always been Igraine's bitch."

Great. Igraine? The last thing I need right now is more names to memorize.

Harris the harasser. Clement the evil Mason. Durgan the marble man. Keith, Mr. Clark Kent. Fin, the peer pressured putz. Alec and Ryan, the mutes. And now Igraine, Keith's master.

My foggy mind isn't up for this.

But it has to be because I have—I have to fight. The alternative is to face the reality of what happened to Aiden, and I'm not strong enough for that.

"The pattern is recognizable," Ryan says.

Damn it, if he's going to start talking more, I'm going to have to find the fucker a different nickname.

"You don't know shit about patterns," Harris spits.

"Speak your mind," Keith encourages him.

"You ain't gonna like it," Ryan answers.

"You alright, Ryan?" Harris asks.

"Sure," Ryan says, his voice calm. "I just don't feel like myself, is all. But the pattern, we've heard about it before. An Archdevil comes in. The Infidel himself orders all his men out. Then the Infidel sends in one of his best. Ares, Endymion, Hades, someone like that. Someone he can be sure can hang with an Archdevil. Before Cris came in, the infidels split. I'm telling you man, he's one of their heavy hitters."

Harris chuckles. "I take my shit back, Ryan. You got it right. What do you say to that, Keith?"

"I'm not saying he's not a heavy hitter." Keith's smile is in his voice.

There is some shifting, and I hear what sounds like a pack being dropped on the floor.

"Fuck it, Alec," Harris says. "You keep your shit quiet. You understand me?"

"Ryan bumped me."

"Ryan didn't bump shit, you fuckhead," Harris snaps.

"Keith," Clement says, his southern accented voice almost giving the man's name two syllables. "What *were* you saying."

"Myla," Durgan's voice cuts through the room. "The whole reason we know we need the Godslayer is because of Myla."

I just can't seem to get away from that bitch. You'd think murdering the woman in cold blood would have been enough to get her out of my life.

Keith laughs. "Right, and she also said that Cris was fresh to Hell when she met him in the City of Blood and Stone. That was all of ten years ago. Certainly not more than fifteen. So if you want to tell me that Cris went from zero to hero in just ten years . . . well, be my guest."

"You laugh at me one more time, motherfucker," Harris says, his voice sounding like he's losing control, "and I don't care who the Order put in charge, I'm going to rip your throat out."

I hear the sound of a blade being drawn from leather.

"Put that shit away, man." Fin's voice is high and weak.

"He wasn't laughing at you, Harris," Clement says. "Was he Fin? He was just laughing."

I hear the snap of a button. It could have been Harris putting away his dagger, but I'm not sure.

"Keith," Harris says. "you better wipe that damn smile off your face, or I'll do it for you."

"Try," Keith answers.

I let my eyes open just slightly. Keith is a demon in the light of the smokeless fire, leaning against the uneven black wall behind him. His face has a rictus grin, a daring grin.

Harris is fuming.

Jesus, what's wrong with these people?

"Less than ten years, as a matter of fact," Durgan's gravelly voice cuts through the tension. "According to Myla, they spent some time together afterwards. I doubt she'd fail to mention any infidel training."

"Then she lied," Alec says. "That fucking bitch lied to us, man. Set us up. She said she was with Xyn, but the whole time that bitch was with the infidels."

If there's one thing Myla was good at, it was pissing people the fuck off.

"Possible," Keith answers, running a hand through his hair where the single white mark marred its otherwise uniform black color. "Then again, Cris could have been an infidel the whole time, and kept it secret from her."

Keith's open mindedness is clearly bothering his compatriots. They seem to need quick, concise answers.

There was a time when I needed the same.

"That's the only explanation that makes a lick of sense," Clement says. "Cris called the shots in Dendra, not El Cid."

"Oh come on," Harris says. "El Cid's name doesn't mean shit to the infidels. Plenty of them could order her around."

This almost makes me snicker. I did indeed take the lead in Dendra. Not because I was in control of Cid, but because my stupid ass didn't know how to behave.

"Whose side are you on?" Clement asks.

"I don't even fucking know, man," Harris says with disgust. "Shit doesn't make any sense."

"Myla may have been deceived," Durgan says, and again, when he speaks, they all become quiet. "But the Godslayer did manage to escape his cell in Maylay Beighlay—somehow. I saw him take a beating which would have immobilized any man. It's possible she was always on his side."

Keith snorts. "You were the one who told us what he did to her. That doesn't *sound* like they were on the same side."

"It's true," Durgan admits. "If that scenario holds,

then their relationship can't have been a pure one."

Well, that's fucking spot on.

"Maybe he got trained in just a few years?" Clement tries.

Keith snorts louder this time. "No one is *that* talented."

"He could've just gotten lucky," Clement says. "Been trained a little, and happened to be chasing after his son."

"No one's that lucky, either," Keith says.

I can't really blame them for skipping right over the truth.

"If it is a deception, boss, we better find out quick," Clement points out.

"Oh, why?" Harris asks.

I hear Keith stand up.

"Because if we tell Igraine we've given her someone who can show her Blood Pass," he says, "and he can't, she might send some Carrion born after us."

Fuck pronouns. Okay, I remember Igraine. That's the woman Keith's all about. But Carrion born? Fuck my damnation. I'm guessing Carrion born are soldiers, but they could be anything. Demons. Corpses. A secret society of angry midgets. Anything.

"That's a good point, Clement," Keith says. "Durgan, I'll need you to extract the information from him before we arrive at Tintagel."

Tintagel? Okay, I'm not even going to try to

remember that one.

"That will be very problematic," Durgan says.

"The hell it will be," Clement argues. "I've seen you tear a man limb from limb. What, you can't break an infidel or something?"

"I can," Durgan says with a cool assurance that sends a spike of fear into my belly. "Infidels break. They might recover faster, but all humans are weak against torture—at least when you can test their claims and return. However, the amount of pain I can inflict on his body, particularly considering how damaged it is right now, must be mitigated lest he be unable to travel."

"Speak English," Clement snaps.

"If we fuck him up too much," Keith translates, "we'll have to carry his ass all the way to Tintagel."

"We might have to now," Harris says.

My skin crawls as if their eyes are on me.

Clement clears his throat. "Now the Godslayer is bound to be smart. Torture will make a man say anything. What if he doesn't know about Blood Pass? What if he just makes shit up?"

Keith snickers. "It doesn't matter if he tells the truth, as long as he says *something*. Igraine's talked to Myla. If Igraine thinks he knows the pass, then we can use him for the trade no matter what."

"We should kill him," Alec says.

Now we're talking.

"And give up a chance to get our hands on that

Angel?" Keith balks.

"He killed God, Keith." Alec's voice is calm for once. "If we trade him away, he's going to escape. He's going to hunt us down and kill us. He's—"

"Watch your words," Durgan says. "I believe the Godslayer is awake."

A shiver runs down my spine.

I hear some shifting, and I open my eyes. Keith is standing over me, his face like a demon's in the pale light of the smokeless fire.

"Don't worry," Keith assures me. "Igraine wants an infidel pet whether or not it comes furnished with the information." He turns, looking to his men. "Durgan, get out there and set up our cover. I don't want his friends following us. When you come back, let's move as far as Lukehold. You can begin torturing the Godslayer there."

I awaken to see Fin hovering over me in the darkness.

The fire has gone out, but there's enough ambient light from the stones of Hell for me to make out his features. There is genuine caring in Fin's eyes. He's the new guy, of that I'm sure. He's a young man, maybe twenty, who hasn't quite yet reached equilibrium age. His eyes are close set under thin eyebrows, and his light hair is curly.

This man shouldn't be in the Order, he's too young. He shouldn't even be in Hell. Or maybe his looks are deceiving and this motherfucker is the most sadistic of them all. Hard to tell.

He's offering me some water. "Drink slowly."

"Fuck your mother, Fin," I say, getting up to my knees.

He chuckles and holds up a bladder of water, not a canteen, mind you, but an actual bladder. Now is it a dyitzu's, a hound's? A human's? I have *no* fucking clue, but right now I wouldn't care if it was St. Pete's bladder, I'm thirsty enough to drink diarrhea.

God that's disgusting. Only I would make myself vomit while nearly dead from dehydration.

I look around to the other hyenas, who for once aren't focused on me. It looks like Durgan isn't back yet.

"Lean your head back when you need a break," Fin says.

He puts the thing's nozzle up to my lips and squeezes. The water fills my mouth and I gulp it down. More's coming, and more after that and more after that. When I lean back to take my lips away, I realize I'm breathing heavily, as if drinking had exhausted me.

"A little more, Godslayer," Fin says.

"I take back everything I ever said about you," I tell him.

And he lets me drink more. I think I like this guy.

Great, I've been captured for one night, and I'm already suffering from Stockholm Syndrome.

"I'd spare you more," Fin says, "but I'm not sure how long it will be until we find water again."

I give him a grin. "Sorry about your God, kid. I didn't mean it."

Well, if I was trying to make a friend, I just ruined the moment. His close-set eyes fill with sorrow. He turns away.

To say religion isn't really my strong point is an understatement on the level of saying there was a slight mix-up on the Hindenburg, so it's hard for me to empathize with this guy. I know there were people back in the old world who loved God truly, like he was another person or something. They had a relationship with the guy. They would see him every Sunday, and call him every night before bed. God was there with them through thick and thin. They'd be overcome with love and emotion and adoration and the light. That religious zeal and ecstasy, it had never been for me—to me, God was that strange aunt who you only remembered on Christmas when she sent you a twenty dollar check enclosed in a Hallmark greeting card—but it must have been for this guy.

Right up until I fucked it for him.

I feel bad, but I don't have an apology left in me.

"It's your own fault, you know," I tell him. "A man's got no business worshiping a devil."

And then, I shit you not, he slaps me. Like he was some kind of bitch. I'm so shocked I must have forgotten to react.

"Wipe that smirk off your face," he says, overcome by emotion, his voice high pitched enough to nail home the illusion that I was talking to a slighted woman from a sixties flick, "Xyn was *not* evil."

"Right," I say. "Maylay Beighlay fell apart from his holiness."

"He destroyed evil institutions." Fin's voice is now loud enough to make me fear he might call in some devils.

"And replaced them with . . ."

He slaps me again, and this time I can't help but laugh.

Suddenly Harris is there, pistol whipping me.

It's a bit harder to laugh that one off.

"You fuck with anyone you want," Harris warns me, nostrils flaring, "but you fuck with Fin again, and I don't care how much you're worth to Keith, I'm going to slaughter you."

"Easy, tiger," I say, "I didn't mean to disturb your lover, and torturing me is Durgan's job, remember."

He flips off the safety.

Please.

Do it.

I can't live anymore.

But dying won't save me from life.

It won't save me from the fact that God sent me to Hell to protect Myla, and I had accomplished the very opposite. In this moment, staring into the gun, I remember when she and I had sat together so long ago on the banks of the river by the brineberry bushes, the both of us crying, holding each other, sobbing as one because of the damage we were doing to ourselves. How can two people want to love each other so much and not be able to?

Durgan's soft voice washes over us all. "He wants to die, Harris."

Harris, sweat droplets on his forehead reflecting the dim light of the chamber, looks toward the marble man.

"I don't know why," Durgan's gravelly voice continues. "Maybe his son died. Maybe his lover." How close Durgan is to the truth scares me. "Maybe it's something else," the wight goes on, "but that man, he wants you to shoot him."

Keith pushes Harris aside, and then pulls away Fin.

"Can you walk?" he asks me.

Harris is literally shaking. No one here is doing well. I knew the Order would be unhealthy, but I didn't think it would be like this. They really are fucked . . . or wait.

Keith's blue eyes look dead inside.

Oh my God.

"You went to Soulfall," I say aloud.

I think of what happened to Neb, of how that place almost destroyed him. Of how it nearly broke Cid. Of how it stole Aiden from me.

These people, they're not just evil and unbalanced, they're soulfucked.

"You did!" I say quickly. "You idiots, you followed

us there? You couldn't have just waited for us to come out?"

"We didn't know," Fin moans. "We didn't know."

Alec begins to cry. Clement starts to console him, putting an arm around his shoulder, but Alec shoves him away.

Durgan's black eyes bore into me.

"Keith," I say, and I'm surprised by how honestly I mean this sentiment, "you had no right to do that to these people."

This evil superman was hurt, and hurt badly. I sense it somehow from his expressionless face, but unlike the others, Keith's too tough to show it.

"I asked if you could walk," he says calmly.

He kneels down beside me and works diligently at the knots on my wrists. The sudden rush of blood into my fingers feels pretty gnarly. It's not so much that it hurts—well, I mean, it does—but the tingling sensation is so different from anything else I've felt that it's hard to classify the feeling as pain.

I stand on my good foot, using the wall for balance. The uneven black rock rubs open a wound I have on my shoulder, but I really can't force myself to care about it. Gingerly, I try putting weight down on my right foot.

It's a lot better than I thought it'd be. I just *feel* like falling to the ground and collapsing from the unearthly agony rather than being forced to. The joint bears my weight. Whatever is fucked up down there isn't going to stop me from walking—and I'm unsure whether that's a blessing or a curse.

Keith cocks one eyebrow.

Tears well in my eyes. "It hurts, but it's stable. Let me wrap it, and I should be able to walk for a few hours."

"Good," Keith says. "Now I know you want to get to Igraine as badly as I do, if only to get out from under my thumb, so I want you to make good decisions about your injury. Don't overwork it, don't underwork it. Can I have your word on that?"

I nod. "You have my word."

Keith's brief smile is meant to convey his understanding of our pact and carries in it no joy or satisfaction. "We're going to retie you in a minute, but we'll cut you loose and arm you if we're attacked, understand?"

I nod again.

"Alright, Fin." Keith hands me a roll of heavy gauze from his pack. "Keep an eye on the Godslayer while he wraps his ankle. When he's done, I want to watch you tie him up. Let's make sure your knots are sound. The last thing we need right now is to go chasing after an escaped infidel with a death wish."

The pain is vaguely intolerable. Each step makes me want to rip into Fin's weak emotional underbelly, but the fucker won't even look at me.

I'd not traveled through these dark halls before, but the natural stone and the sudden strobes of the Erebus' blue lightning gives me a sense of déjà vu.

I look behind me often, hoping against hope . . . but Hell's the wrong place for hope.

Fortunately our progress is slow because I don't think I could keep up otherwise.

We stop in a small black chamber with red crystals emerging from the rock. My foot throbs incessantly into the tight gauze, and it sucks, but it sure as hell beats walking. I prop my leg up on a rock jutting out from the wall and hope like hell elevating my ankle will help.

Keith and Durgan kneel, whispering to each other. I close my eyes and do my best to listen.

"Too many," Durgan is saying.

"He's not slowed us up so far, but I doubt he'll be able to run," Keith says.

I keep my eyes shut and face impassive. I hear a whistling in my mind, strong enough for me to think it might be hellsong. It's the whistle a boy might make as he walks nonchalantly away from a broken vase.

I'm not eavesdropping, Keith, just keep on talking.

"A lot of your men probably can't," Durgan says coldly. "I'll leave you at the far end of the falls. The noise from the water should give you camouflage from the senses of the devils. I'll find a free path, and we'll attempt to cross."

"And you're sure the infidels won't be able to follow us?"

"Correct. Even Ares' huntsmen would have difficulty breaching such a widespread pack of dyitzu."

"But not you," Keith says, and I hear amusement in his voice.

"But not me."

I open my eyes, hearing movement beside me. It's Ryan. I'm not sure what to think of his mental state. He was completely lucid in their earlier conversation about me, but now he seems dazed somehow. Maybe lost. In any event, while he's quiet, he appears not to care about what's going on. Maybe he's in some kind of shock, some kind of disassociation triggered by the horrors of Soulfall.

As he passes I notice some of the skin on his right cheek is peeling, mute evidence he'd gotten a little too close to a dyitzu fireball.

The whole group is moving, so I shuffle back to my feet, de-elevating my leg. The blood rushing down into my foot presses my wounded ankle fiercely back into the gauze and Jessica's boot.

Mother-fucking-mother-fuckity-fuck-fuck.

The next couple rooms are an agony, but as we move my extremity loosens and the pain becomes merely a fuckity-fuck-fuck.

There is a low rumble I begin to feel as much as hear, and I wonder if perhaps it's another form of hellsong. But no, now I recognize it. It's the river, the Northern Lethe, traveling in a rush above our heads.

If I could climb up a few hundred feet, I could follow that river back to Portsmouth, Dendra and Maylay Beighlay.

But why? Why would I bother.

There is no one left for me there.

In the next couple rooms the rumbling gets louder, and I feel the moisture in the air. The dark, natural stone becomes slick with condensation, and the dewy drops of water give the shine of the embedded crystals a little extra zest.

Ahead, a passage beckons, the blue of the lightning calling us forth, mixing its illumination with the red crystals and filling the tunnel with a purple color that reminds me of Q's sword. Aiden has that sword, my lonely and lost Aiden. The son I could not save.

The rush of the Lethe becomes deafening as we enter the low passage. The ceiling is only four feet tall, so we have to duck as we make our way through. I'm right behind Fin, and Clement is right behind me. I consider trying to fight them, bound hands be damned, in the tight confines. But I'm injured, and tired, and outnumbered, and . . . broken.

I hear Keith talking up ahead, but the sound of the river is so loud I can't make out his words.

Then the passage opens up, not to the Lethe, but to the Erebus.

It is perversely beautiful.

The ledge we're standing on is tucked into a ravine on the eternal cliff which marks our side of the river of darkness. It's perhaps twenty feet wide and thirty feet long. I see and comprehend this twisted river of Hell—made of evil air rather than water—as it rushes between the two infinite rock faces. Streams of slow lightning form tangled webs of blue energy, pulsing and writhing in the effervescent flow of ire. The view, so mighty, is framed by the rising rock around me, but the obstructions lie at the very edges of my vision, so it doesn't seem to lessen the grandeur of this terrible hellscape.

I limp forward, peering across the dim river, seeing through its miasma to the far cliff. Between these two cliffs, of course, I can see Soulfall. The sight of the place sends a shiver up my spine. Of all my friends, I had faced the least mental damage from the nightmarish realities that echoed our own fears and insecurities. That was okay though, I'd brought my own mental doom to Soulfall in the form of my son.

Sometimes I feel . . . like a motherless child.

The rushing sound is coming from what is perhaps the largest waterfall I've ever seen. I'd forgotten the river Cid led us down was merely an offshoot of the great Northern Lethe. This is the real beast. Its wide waters, thicker than Niagara, rocket out into the river of darkness as an ancient sailor might have imagined the oceans doing at the end of the world.

Down, down, down the waters plummet into the infinite abyss of damnation. There is no lake where they fall, though the river has dug wide juts into the bedrock beside us, laying bare abandoned beds of whetstone where its previous courses must have taken it.

"Get a lasso around the Godslayer," Keith shouts above the torrent of water. "And keep him away from the edge."

Obediently, Fin gets a rope around me and guides me to the wall.

Durgan and Keith share a nod, and the wight heads back into the passage.

I hate that wight. I want to kill him. To kick him off the cliff so he can fall forever. But right now, and just for right now, I wish him luck. If he fails to scout well, then we'll be set upon by masses of dyitzu.

I realize that's not really what I want. Why? Why don't I want to die? Is it because I fear Sheol? Is it because some part of me is too stupid to realize I've nothing left to live for?

I decide to stop letting my brain itch at these thoughts. It's better that way because at the end of this hall of questions, I'm sure, is the knowledge that truly, fundamentally, I don't want to live.

Using my bound hands to help me, I lower myself to the floor and again prop up my wounded ankle, trying hard not to think how badly it's going to hurt when I stand again.

I want to close my eyes, but the brilliant blue light doesn't really care if they're shut or not. For a while, I try covering my eyelids with my forearm, but eventually I just stare at the river and let its hypnotic flow take my mind along with it.

"Holy shit," Clement shouts above the rushing waters. "Oh fuck, man. Look there! On Soulfall."

"Keep away from the edge," Keith shouts back.

Harris moves to grab Clement.

"Look!" Clement shouts back at Harris, pointing

toward Soulfall.

Harris grabs Clement's arm—but then stops.

"Keith," Harris says. "You better come take a look at this."

Whatever it is, I have to see it. I get up slowly, cursing inwardly as I lower my ankle. It's so stiff I'm forced to use the cliff wall to keep my balance.

Fin, holding the rope he'd tied around my waist firmly, follows along, giving me less slack than you'd give a disobedient dog—but at least he's letting me go look.

Fin doesn't let me get any closer than five feet or so from the ledge, but I think I can see what Clement is going on about.

There's a room on the side of Soulfall who's wall is made of glass. Inside, there's a man beating furiously at the window. It's hard to get much detail from this distance, but that man is frantic. My heart goes out to him.

He stops for a moment, looking over one shoulder as if something's coming for him, and then renews his efforts on the glass.

He's darkly dressed. I know from overhearing the hyenas' conversations that they'd lost a few men, and that certainly looks like one of their guys. They'd abandoned him. Not even a cancer man deserves that.

But wait. He seems especially familiar.

Everyone around me is looking at Ryan, and I

realize why.

With surprise, I compare the two men, the Ryan next to me, and the distant Ryan trapped behind the glass.

Durgan's voice startles me because I didn't know he'd returned. "It's Soulfall," he says. "It knows you've been there. It's trying to call you back."

Whatever weird state of shock has been protecting Ryan gives way—his eyes are wide and full of horror.

"We've got to go back," he says quickly.

Fin jerks at the suggestion and even Harris' face blanches with fear.

"We ain't going back there, man!" Clement shouts.

"It's not you," Keith tries to reason with Ryan. "It's an illusion."

Ryan looks left and right, as if searching for enemies in our midst. "You're wrong!" And he bolts for the cliff.

Harris jumps forward, and catches him, keeping him from the ledge.

"You're wrong," Ryan screeches, struggling against Harris' arms. "I knew it. I knew it. I left something behind! We have to go back. Don't you understand? That's me. That's the real me! Look!"

The other Ryan seems to have spotted us, and though he'd been frantic before, that was nothing compared to the inane fury he's possessed with now.

He throws himself into the glass, arms whirling,

head-butting, clawing, kicking and punching. His mouth is open, though his screams can't reach our ears. Something is darkening the window, perhaps his blood.

I look back to our Ryan, the real Ryan, and I want to comfort him. I want to take him up in my arms like Harris has and whisper into his soul that it will all be okay.

And maybe I could do that, if my hands were untied.

And maybe it would help.

But I bet all I'd really accomplish is to make myself a liar.

"Come," Durgan's voice rumbles against the rush of the waterfall. "We haven't much time."

VII

The pace Durgan sets through the wilds is frustratingly sporadic, and the toll it's taking on my ankle is severe. As we move quickly through the architect worked halls, I'm forced to increasingly favor my right leg. My bound hands aren't doing anything to help my balance, and I start catching myself against the walls with my cut up shoulder.

On the bright side, I'm leaving a blood trail for Q to follow—or any devil that's near.

After each hurried jog, Durgan has us crouch down in small rooms, and then, after brief solo scouting missions, returns to take us away again. As a wight, the dyitzu won't attack him, but they sure as hell won't spare us on his account.

Our rest periods are so short I give up elevating my leg.

"Keith," I whisper at our next stop, "my ankle is about to give."

Keith let's out a long sigh. "Durgan says we're nearly at the Carrion. We've got a safe room there. Can you make another three dashes?"

"I can."

Fin looks at me, worry in his eyes.

Apparently he still likes me even after I insulted his God. Well, come to think of it, I killed his God, but what really pissed him off was me rubbing his face in it. I start to feel a bit guilty. Sure, of the thousands of gods men had worshiped over the years, he picked the absolute worst one available, but Xyn is dead now. Why make Fin feel worse than he already does?

Durgan returns. "We've got a decision to make."

"Go on," Keith says.

"There is a long hallway that seems deserted, but it is highly problematic. I didn't see any devils at the entrance, but it is a ten mile loop, so there could be some in there. We can stay low to minimize our profile, and we only have to pass through about half of it, but the nature of the place means anyone anywhere along the hallway should be able to detect us as we move.

"Choice number two is to go low and use a series of crawlways. The progress will be much slower."

Keith looks to me. "If your life depended on it, could you run a mile?"

I think about this.

"Yes," I say, "but only if my life depended on it."

Keith shrugs. "The loop it is."

Hell never stops surprising me.

The ceiling of Durgan's hallway is full of black crystals, and they are as dark as whetstone. For some reason, when we walk, our vibrations run up the wall to the crystals and, as they shake, they begin to emit a dull red light. On our left wall is glass, which reminds me of the window we'd just seen on Soulfall. The floor and the remaining wall of our passage are made of charcoal grey hellstone bricks.

When I look through the glass, I see that our corridor curves around a hollowed-out cylinder. The cylinder goes up and down for about a mile, and the only interruption in its bricked surface is our window. The window runs seamlessly along the left side of our hallway.

Jesus.

"Once we start down this path," Durgan says, "we won't be able to change course without backtracking. That means anyone who comes in after us, and anyone who might be hiding in there now, will be able to see us all the way around." His finger points along our future path through the miles-long curved glass wall.

Keith motions to the ceiling. "And the crystals light up the whole way?"

Durgan nods. "Yes."

I notice even the vibrations of our voices creates tiny little pinpricks of light on the tips of the crystals. If there is anyone in the hallway, they surely can see the red flickering above us.

We watch through the window, looking for any signs of lit crystals.

"There's a stream past our exit," Durgan says. "We'll clean ourselves there to rid our scent. Then we'll rest in the Carrion."

That seems like the wrong order to do things, actually. We should rest here, then wash, then go into the Carrion. But Hell, it's their show, and if there's a simple reason why I'm wrong, I'd rather not let them know how stupid I am.

We walk as softly as possible, but even so, tiny red lights flash along the ceiling above. When one of us makes a misstep, the light is bright enough to bathe us in its bloodlike color.

"This is insane," Alec mutters.

Keith grunts in agreement. "The Devil is a bastard," he says. "He'll give you a shortcut, but he sure as hell is going to make you pay for it."

My ankle starts to feel better at the midway point, but that doesn't last. As we continue along the barely-curved hallway, the swelling begins to come back. Tears of pain are starting to form in my eyes.

"I need to rewrap my ankle," I say.

Durgan takes a long look through the window, probably searching for any red lights. "You must hurry," he warns.

"Quickly, Godslayer," Keith says.

I drop to my butt and hold up my hands. Fin works hard at the knots. Seeing his lack of progress, however, Keith leads him aside.

"You didn't teach me how to *untie* it," Fin explains.

Keith's blue eyes stare at me intently as he kneels down beside me. Fin turns around with the others to look through the window, and suddenly I'm having a private moment with Keith.

"Why does Cid hate you?" I ask.

Keith ignores the question. He works quickly at the rope, and I realize I'll soon be free.

"What did you see in Soulfall?" Keith asks so softly that the crystals barely sparkle above us.

With a flash of insight I realize that Keith is almost as much a prisoner as I am. Harris had mentioned that Keith was assigned these men by the Order. They don't follow him out of admiration but out of fear and respect for the organization. If Keith ever failed to live up to that ideal, they would have no problems turning their backs on him.

And maybe that's what I want, or maybe it isn't. Keith, for all his evil intent, is at least reasonable. The others are as emotional as Myla.

"It hurt us," I say. "Even Cid. It broke a couple of us."

Keith finishes with the ropes, but he doesn't move away. As far as his men know, he's still working.

"Did you feel like there was something," he says, "something . . ."

"From below," I finish for him. "An evil force. A cruel mind."

Keith nods fervently, his eyes wide, and it seems like he wants to look back toward his men, but is afraid to do so. "I think it . . . did it, did you get the feeling that it . . ."

This time I don't know what he means. "It what?"

"I think it came out with—"

"We've got company," Harris says.

"Quiet," Durgan warns.

"I don't see nothin'," Clement whispers.

I quickly unwrap my ankle. The joint is pretty damn swollen. I breathe in through my teeth. Fuck. I am so fucked.

"There," Harris says, putting a finger on the glass. "Right back by the beginning."

Together, the hyenas stare through the window.

"I see it," Ryan says.

Alec starts shaking. Then he pisses himself.

Jesus.

"Confirmed," Durgan agrees. "We're being

followed."

"You said the infidels couldn't keep up with us." Alec's soft voice shakes, like his body, with his anxiety.

I smell his urine.

"They didn't," Durgan assures him. "I led them astray long enough for us to find where Cris fell, remember? No, most likely it is dyitzu on our trail."

I really hate this fucking wight. I'd hated Keith before, because he'd been the one I'd thought had got the Order chasing me, but now I'm starting to think it's Durgan who is the main culprit.

I begin to wrap my ankle, working quickly, but not *too* quickly. I wonder if Durgan is lying. If so, then even though his face is half turned away, those black eyes could be focused on me. Maybe he's judging whether I bought his lie or not.

Well, liar or no, I can at least figure out if he's looking at me.

I give a slight upward nod and make a couple of kisses at him.

His face turns toward me. "Quickly, Godslayer."

I grin.

Rationally, I don't know that it's my friends on our tail, but I imagine Q, leading Cid and Neb, weaving his way around the traps Durgan has set for them.

Please be you, brother. I need you more than ever.

VIII

As we leave the long hallway, I cast one long look over my shoulder, hoping to see red lights twinkling in the distance.

I don't.

They untie me again when we arrive at some random river. It's only about ten feet wide and ten feet deep, and the water travels quickly along its squared-off banks.

They begin to strip.

Infidels don't have body shame, but I'm not really an infidel yet, so I'm going to have to fake it.

My shame lessens upon seeing their wiry, malnourished bodies. Ribs stick out from their thin forms. Harris is broader than most, and Fin is smoother, but model specimens of masculinity they are not.

Durgan is interesting to look at. The illusion that his skin looks like marble is intensified by his nudity. In a way, he seems almost like an old statue, the kind Myla used to liken me too. Keith, however, is one strong motherfucker. I notice this as I drop to my ass to unwrap my foot. His body looks more like an infidel's than those around him. His shoulders are both lean and full. His abdomen, perhaps not quite a six pack, shows good definition.

I disrobe from my sitting position, and though I'm careful, taking off my pants twinges my left ankle.

Fuck.

Wounded though I am, I find I'm proud of my body. I don't let my gaze linger on my nakedness for too long, because while infidels may not have body shame, they sure as hell aren't narcissists.

I scoot on my butt toward the river, using my good foot and both hands. Keith tosses my clothes and the shoes Jessica'd made me across the way.

I miss my pack and my Old Lady. I hope Cid and Q still have them.

The water is oh so bloody cold.

Jesus effing Christ.

With an effort that I would have thought beyond me, I slip into the water as if it is a summer stream.

A few of the other hyenas have already appeared

on the far side, shivering and dripping, their balls receding up into their pubic hair.

They are dipping their clothes into the stream and then wringing them out. Hopefully that will lessen our scent for the hounds and dyitzu in the Carrion.

The Carrion is where the City of Blood and Stone is. I remember those areas being horrifying.

Fin is nice enough to dip my clothes into the river and begins washing my stink out. That's nice of him.

I emerge as best I can, and stand on one leg, willing my body not to shiver.

It doesn't.

Go you, body, go you. Shame these evil motherfuckers. Who says good can't be pretty?

We dry ourselves by running the water off our limbs with our hands, which I'm forced to do from a sitting position. Then, as they clothe themselves, I begin wrapping my foot. The way Harris stares at me is creepy in the high school gym teacher kind of way. What a weirdo.

I have to admit that the brief jaunt into the water has made them look a bit more lively. I feel it too. The cold water has my blood pumping through my veins like a fresh spring. The river could have done more to lessen the swelling around my ankle, surely, but who am I to complain?

Ryan, however, looks much worse for the wear. The water has puckered up the peeling skin on the right side of his face. Those burns are far worse than I thought.

"Quickly," Durgan says. "The Carrion is close, and we can be assured the dyitzu will not be able to follow us there."

Dyitzu? Or Q? Which is it you're afraid of, Durgan?

"We shouldn't go back into the Carrion," Alec says.

Keith snorts. "We have to."

"Why?"

And I realize that right now, they need me. They need me badly. I'm something to do. I'm a mission. They're hurting so much from Soulfall that they *have* to have something to do. Without me, they are just lost little soldiers. Without me, all the horrors they suffered in those dark halls in the middle of the Erebus will have been for nothing.

"Shut the hell up, Alec," Harris tells him.

After I'm clothed, I stand and test my foot again.

Oh man. Oh, totally shit hell man.

"I don't have long," I warn them.

Durgan's black eyes flash as he turns to me. "You won't need long."

Finally our pace is even, and I can't pretend I miss all the furtive starting and stopping. That being said, I don't see much of a future in walking for me. At some point, I'm going to have to let this ankle heal.

When I lean against the walls for balance, I can tell

that the stones around us are getting cooler, and it's not long before the air does the same. The chill is nothing like the pole, but it's enough to make goosebumps pop up on my skin. The light, which has been ridiculously dim this entire time, changes in color, often covering the hyenas in a soft, purple-hued light. At other times, I see yellow illuminated cubbies. The ceilings get lower, and occasionally we have to duck to avoid hitting our heads on the strange archways.

I see a purple marker stone which I remember serves to warn us that we're very, very near to the Carrion.

"The ancients walled the Carrion off, it was so bad," Keith tells us.

"Pussies," Harris jokes, but no one laughs.

Well, except me, but I'm not exactly who you'd consider his target audience.

Gingerly, we walk down the passage. There was a barrier here, but something had burst through it. Judging from how much the stone debris had been absorbed, much of it appearing as if it was half melted into the floor and wall, I'd guess whatever breached the barrier did so several decades ago.

"I don't want to go in there," Alec says from behind me.

Harris places a hand on the remaining stonework. Whoever built this barrier had quarried the stone from nearby, that much seems certain. They'd locked the bricks together with some kind of mortar. Maybe it was ground up hellstone. Maybe the ancients did build a barrier here, long ago, but this doesn't seem like their work. Of course, I'm no expert.

Some of the bricks, each the size of my head, were split in two, and half-healed cracks spread through the barrier and into the architect-built wall it's attached to.

The breach is easily large enough for a man to fit through.

"I'm not going into the Carrion," Alec insists.

Keith, who'd nearly stepped through the barrier, turns back, a quizzical look on his face. "We've got to, man. Don't you want to get your hands on that Angel? Don't you know what the Order will give us?"

Alec shakes his head, closing his eyes tightly.

"I don't care," he whines.

Harris and I give simultaneous sighs of disgust.

"Jinx," I say, but Harris isn't amused.

Durgan cocks his head to one side, his black eyes studying Alec carefully.

"Don't you understand?" Alec shouts.

The hairs stand up on the back of my neck.

"Pipe down!" Clement's harsh whisper is almost as loud as Alec's shout was. "We're just outside the Carrion, you idiot."

Alec shakes his head back and forth, his nostrils flaring with each intense breath. "We can't take it back with us."

Is he talking about me?

Keith's voice is soft but oh-so-concerned. "Take what back with us, Alec?"

"We must go, and quickly," Durgan says. "It's not safe to stay here."

"You heard him, Alec," Clement says. "No dallying. Get your ass in gear, soldier."

Alec draws a pistol and points it at Clement. "I'm not going."

Clement freezes.

"Whoa, whoa, whoa, whoa!" Harris says, raising his hands in the air.

Other than Clement, only Durgan and myself fail to step back. Me, because I'd have to hop, and I assume the marble man just doesn't care because his stonewight ass is immune to bullets.

"We didn't know you felt this strongly about it," Keith says. "Point the gun down. Let's sit and talk. We'll have a little powwow. You can tell us what you mean and we can work this out."

Alec looks left and right. "It's with us," he squeaks, his face seeming for all the world like a lost child's. "*He's* with us."

"It's okay," Keith says. "We're safe now. We just need to get to Tintagel and we can rest. We can heal our wounds, our mental wounds. But we have to make it there first."

Alec blows his brains out so quickly I don't even

jerk in shock until after parts of his skull hit the ceiling and the wall behind him. His lifeless form falls, knees hitting first before face planting into the ground.

I look to the faces of the hyenas. Even Keith is fucked up, and it's Durgan alone who remains impassive.

Only now do I realize how deeply Soulfall damaged them. They really do need me—and then, with the terror of a personal epiphany that can only come when you accidently discover a thing you've hidden from yourself, I realize I need them every bit as much.

Wordlessly, we enter the Carrion.

Well, Q, if you really are back there, brother, you can't say I didn't leave you a nice trail.

After five minutes in the Carrion, I find I'm mentally exhausted.

The air is cold and for some reason that makes my ankle ache all the more. With my intellectual faculties drained, I no longer have the fortitude to ignore the burning agony shooting up through my leg.

Brilliant lights shine out from distant cubbies, doing almost nothing to illuminate the black nightmare around us, but easily destroying my night vision. The ceiling is about ten feet above us, but the chambers are so large, perhaps half a mile wide and similarly deep, they seem oppressive. Visibility here is absolute shit. Pillars and walls, arches and barricades, they all rise up from the floor to meet the low ceiling, blocking our vision in the short term while the darkness swallows all in the distance.

We could be in the center of an army of dyitzu and not know it.

The long lights turn our shadows into living things, and the different sources cause us all to jump here and there as the dark shapes of our friends, their forms discombobulated by the sharp angle of the illumination, quickly cross our paths.

This place is a God damned nightmare.

Durgan leads us carefully forward, and everyone has their shotguns at the ready. Everyone but me. I stretch my hands against the rope to test my bonds, but there's no give at all.

We pass under an arch that leads us into the next chamber, and I notice it has a violet keystone at its top.

Perhaps that is why the ancients chose purple hellstone to mark off the Carrion.

We take a left turn, and then a right, and then we walk across another half-mile chamber. I think I'm about to faint from the pain, but then Durgan turns back, his black eyes glistening in the distant light of some far-off cubby.

"We're here," the wight says.

And we follow him to yet another arch, but this one has a double door. I don't know whether this door was made by man or the architect, but its woodstone seems very ancient indeed. In the place of handles, it has the carved stone heads of lions. Carefully, Durgan reaches his hand into the maw of one head and pulls open the door. The hinges are completely silent.

A wind blows fiercely from within, and its howling causes the muscles in my back to stiffen with fear.

The wight leads us in, and my heart sinks.

This room is epic in scale, perhaps several times the size of an old world football stadium. Rising for perhaps half a mile are tiered levels, set up almost like bleachers, each about twenty feet tall. Wide stone stairways lead up at even intervals, providing access to the rising tiers. Along the face of each tier are yawning openings, about fifty or so between each set of steps. Altogether, there seems to be thousands of exits from this chamber. Unless I leave a good sign for Q, there is no way even a tracker of his skill would know which path to follow.

Good god.

"Pick one, Keith," Durgan says. "I'll keep my eyes on Cris. If any of the dyitzu do follow us into the Carrion, they'll lose us here. Short of a hound, our path will be untraceable."

Dyitzu my ass. Would Durgan take such a precaution to avoid dyitzu? Maybe, but I'm betting my friends are on our tail.

Keith takes us left along the room and leads us up the stairs. I want to drop a piece of hair, or drip some blood, or something, but Durgan is following right behind me, and who knows what those black eyes see. Often he stops, and when he does, the others pause, giving him time to pick up whatever tiny bit of detritus we've left behind.

And even if he misses something, I realize, the wind would soon scatter our trail anyway.

Honestly, I think even Hansel and Gretel would be fucked right now.

We walk into one of the myriad entrances, and I realize this is some sort of catacomb. Bones, stripped bare of flesh in what I guess is an attempt to ensure they do not rise as corpses, are sometimes entombed in clear crystal. In other areas, entire enclaves have been devoted to store the piles of bones.

How many lie here?

The howling of the wind becomes distant, and the gusts which muss my hair and cool my skin become more and more infrequent. Then Durgan leads us to a half-empty enclave.

"Here," he says. "We may sleep among the bones."

In the cold, surrounded by the dangers of the Carrion, with the sounds of the whipping wind, I doubt many men could sleep here comfortably . . . but I'm so tired, I care not for the blasphemy I commit against my ancestors as I fall down upon the bones . . . and like a babe, I sleep.

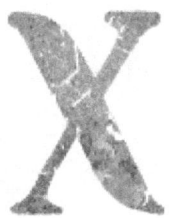

I awaken to the smell of devilwheat. Normally, my hands would have been tied behind my back, but they are still bound in front of me as they'd not retied them last night. I shift, disturbing the skulls which double for my pillow and the ribcage which I had—and believe me, this grosses me out more than it does you—been cuddling with in my sleep.

Sorry buddy, I hope you were into that kind of thing before you died.

With my bound hands, I push aside the ribs like an unwanted hooker and check out my ankle.

On a scale from one to FUBAR, my ankle is on the far side of the US Congress. Well, maybe it's exactly like

Congress. I can make some slow progress with it, but an amputation would probably speed me up.

Dry bones crunch under Keith's booted feet—and I remember how quietly this man can move when he wants to. Of the hyenas, he's the one most like an infidel, but even so, Soulfall is weighing on his shoulders—and there is no one here who can support him, not really.

Only me.

"You awake, Godslayer?" he asks.

"Damned and ready."

"We have some food we're going to feed you, and some water, but you won't be allowed to piss or shit for another mile. Think you can handle that?"

I think I can, but I don't want to betray his trust without good reason.

"I'm not sure," I tell him.

"Can you stand?" he asks, looking at my ankle.

Somewhere, in the depths of my being, I get the sudden feeling I should give up. There's no reason to fight. My son's gone. My friends won't be able to follow me. I failed my one mission from God. I'm just . . .

"You don't know," Keith states.

It's as good an answer as any, I suppose.

"Feed him now," Keith orders back over his shoulder.

"Aye, sir," Fin answers.

Keith does me the honor of untying me so I can

feed myself.

I am both ravenous and not hungry. That must mean I'm depressed. Which means my wounds will heal slowly. Which means . . .

As mechanically as I have ever done anything, I eat.

Again I hold my wrists flat together to have them tied in front of me.

It strikes me as odd that they didn't retie my hands last night. It's a pretty damn bad sign that I didn't even consider escaping. If I could somehow be healthy, and not mentally fucked, I'd be able to take advantage of the plight of my captors.

And as an infidel, it's my duty to be that strong.

But I'm not.

And I can't help but admit that.

Keith and Fin help me up from the bones, and I realize that, in the mess of skeletons, I can't identify the one that kept me company last night.

Putting my wounded foot down on the uneven bones is a level of excruciating agony I would have thought was only reserved for eyes or genitals. Got to give some credit to my ankle, it's really stepped up its pain game today.

My eyes water as I hop out of the bone enclave. My stomach is already rumbling, and I feel some pressure on my asshole. I'm not horribly sure whether I want to shit myself or not. Fortunately, the adrenalin rush caused by my next limping footstep seems to tighten everything up.

The hyenas must not have eaten much lately either because they're farting pretty seriously. I giggle out loud as I imagine Q tracking us by scent. Of course, that's impossible, but it's funny to me all the same.

"Whatchya laughin' at, boy?" Clement asks.

"All I got was devilwheat," I say. "I didn't know you guys ate the beans."

Ryan looks at me oddly. "You are the queerest infidel I've ever met."

His face is an absolute mess. Somehow it looks even worse than yesterday.

"You catch something from the dead guy you slept with last night?" I ask him.

"Fuck you."

Clement snickers.

"Don't let the Infidel Friend get under your skin," Harris warns Ryan.

"I wouldn't dare go under his skin," I shoot back, "that shit looks fucked up."

Clement snickers again.

Ryan doesn't seem angry, but he does appear to be deeply confused. What the hell is he thinking about?

The hallway is insanely long. On either side, enclaves open up, little dugouts full of bones. The numbers of the dead here are mindboggling, particularly considering how many paths there were leading out of the stadium chamber. Could they all be so full of bones?

My ankle limbers a little as we go, but as the pain recedes, my need to shit returns. Fortunately, I'm not alone in this regard.

"We far enough to piss yet?" Fin asks.

"Yes," Durgan answers.

"Little help?" I ask, offering my bonds forward.

Ryan goes to untie me but after a few attempts, can't. What's worse is that, unlike Fin, he doesn't even seem to know where to start. At first I think he's getting some petty revenge, but the look of consternation on his face is so complete I begin to suspect he's earnest.

Man, Soulfall has these people good and deeply messed up.

He leaves to go shit in the bone pile.

Keith eventually returns and lets me free.

I accept the pain of hobbling into the next enclave, a fresh enclave, before beginning to relieving myself.

I squat amongst the bones.

". . . that's bullshit!" Clement's uncontrolled voice reaches me from the next enclave. "You saw him blow his brains out, right there in front of us."

Whoever he's talking to hushes him harshly. I cock my head to one side and listen, but their whispers are just too soft.

It does not take long, though, before Clement gets

agitated again.

"Of *course* it was suicide!" he says.

Fin's voice is the one that replies, equally agitated. "I'm telling you, I felt it. It's following us. It's driving us crazy, one by one. Ryan's probably next. We're cursed. I think that's why Keith is pushing so hard to get us to the Angel—"

Their quiet voices are interrupted by Harris' sharp words. "I can't hear myself shit. Keep it down."

They become silent.

They'd mentioned that Angel before, but it can't really be a white-robed, harp and wings Angel, can it? How much of that Christian mythology is actually true?

I ponder this while I try my best to shit.

My ankle swells into its wraps every time I push, which is annoying. The first part of my bowel movement is almost constipated, but the remainder is fairly explosive.

"Guess you got the beans too, huh?" Harris mocks me, and I'm surprised to see he's moved to the hallway.

I feel like I should have some barbed quip ready to fire back at him, but I don't, so I let his comment pass.

I use someone's rib to scrape clean my asshole.

Then I hear a sharp intake of breath from the next enclave.

"Oh," Clement says.

"I know. I know." Fin's words hang for a moment in the cold Carrion air.

"I believe you." Clement's whisper is forlorn.

I feel my back tense in fear. The hell does Fin know that I don't?

Harris' eyes narrow. "Quickly, Godslayer."

I limp out of the enclave.

Fin is there, eyes red as if he's been crying. His hands shake as he ties my wrists up.

Harris glares at me, as if daring me to take advantage of Fin's vulnerable state.

My eyes bore into Fin's face, hoping for some clue as to the context of his conversation, but all I see in him is terror.

Then we're off, and all I'm left with is a sense of foreboding deep in my stomach.

It's following us. Fin had said. *It's driving us crazy, one by one.*

After a mile, my ankle just won't support me anymore.

"Keith," I say. "I have done my best. I can no longer walk."

He looks sad.

Durgan comes to me and then stomps on my ankle.

I don't remember falling, but I'm on the ground, tears pouring out of my eyes.

Clement is laughing a high pitched yet quiet laugh. "Not so funny now, are you?"

I want to kill him. He's a shithead, he's worth nothing. A stupid motherfucking redneck. He has no right to laugh at me.

Why? Why had Durgan done this?

Because now that I can't walk, he doesn't need to worry about damaging me anymore. They have to carry me anyway.

Fuck.

Fuck fuck fuck.

Like a sack of potatoes, Durgan hoists me up from the floor and tosses me across his shoulders in a fireman's carry. He makes no effort to avoid bumping my ankle against the walls.

I cry out in pain. Surely that will make him stop. He can't afford any nearby demons hearing me.

Durgan speaks quietly. "Shout not, Godslayer. Do so again, and I'll remove your ability to shout with my knife."

Cid, please save me. Please.

Sometimes I feel . . . like a motherless child.

I don't know if we're close enough to the Erebus for shared hellsong, or if this is just the normal effect from the distant howling winds of the stadium chamber behind us, but I hear the notes clearly.

And sometimes I feel . . . like a motherless child.

I have to start memorizing each chamber and path if I'm to have any hope.

But now that I'm being carried, it's much harder to pay attention. I make a compromise with myself and agree to memorize the veins . . . but even so, I have to admit I probably won't remember any of this.

Ryan stops them all.

"What's wrong, Ryan?" Keith asks.

"Harpy den," he responds.

Durgan grunts. "Not so. It has been abandoned for some time."

I look up to see Ryan and notice just how bad his peeling face looks.

Poor motherfucker.

"I smell something," Ryan mentions.

Durgan bends his head back and sniffs. "Pomegranate."

"Sounds tasty," Fin says, and I shit you not, I hear his stomach rumble.

Durgan shakes his head. "It might be enough to obscure the scent of harpies. Ryan's right, we should go around."

They all stare at Durgan. How often has he been wrong? How often has Ryan been right? Something about this exchange must be very odd to elicit such a reaction.

Durgan manages to crack my ankle against a wall on the way out, and I almost lose consciousness.

I start thinking of information I can trade them for a reprieve.

I sicken myself because as soon as I think of something convincing, lie or not, I'm going to give it to them. I'm supposed to be an infidel, and I shouldn't, but I'm going to.

Q isn't coming.

There is no way he could track me through the stadium chamber.

I've lost faith in my ability to save myself, and no one's coming for me.

I don't have a ton of experience with this crippling self-doubt thing—or rather, when I'd experienced it before, I'd had a sufficient amount of denial on hand to push through it. I'm not sure if I've become more adept at avoiding my own self-deception, or if the complete and total nature of just how unbelievably fucked I am is more than my poor animal brain can handle.

Probably the latter.

Whelp, looks like I'll just have to step up my game.

You've got this, buddy. You're skilled. You're smart. Everyone thinks you're handsome. I believe in you, Cris. Be the ball. Don't let a little damnation get you down. We're not going to take it anymore.

Now why the Hell didn't I get that for hellsong?

I need an intermediate goal. Something that I might be able to achieve in the next few hours. Something that would raise my morale.

Durgan rams my head into a stone wall as we pass through an arch—just hard enough to hurt like hell, but not quite hard enough to make much noise.

He's strangely attentive to details like that.

Something. I've got to do something.

Something like strangling Durgan to death. Wights need to breathe, don't they? Hell, I don't know. Corpses breathe, but they don't *need* to breathe—I've definitely seen a few without lungs. He doesn't seem to sweat but blood goes to his head, right? A choke cuts off a person's blood supply, and the black ichor which runs through his veins probably brings something to his brain, even if it's not oxygen.

The truth is I don't know if you can choke a wight, but there is only one way to find out. The infidels are all about empiricism. Observe and record your results. I'll choke that fucker until his face turns . . . well more white than it is right now. And then, if he dies, great. If not, I'll hammer his head in with a rock. That I *know* kills a wight.

"Easy on our prisoner," Keith says. "I know he can't run right now, but he probably could to save his life. We don't want to do too much damage."

I am suddenly grateful, and very suspicious. I know Keith doesn't necessarily like all these guys. Is he planning to break from them? Also, where the hell was that suggestion two hours ago?

Better late than never, I guess.

Ryan is shedding some hair, and Durgan steps over it.

I can practically feel how pissed off the wight is right now. Infidels aren't the only things that could be wandering around in the Carrion, of course, and I'm sure plenty of demons would want to track us down and murder us.

The shedding is a good sign for Ryan though. Dude was taking a while to heal, but losing that hair probably means the last of his burnt skin is peeling off.

The path Durgan is taking us along seems rather peculiar. The passages we choose don't always lead us in the same direction, and the odd stairs and depressions we traverse appear random. At times he stops, lets me down, and scouts ahead. I shudder to think how we would have made it without him. Honestly, we probably couldn't. Often we pass along ridges where we can hear our enemies above or below us, usually hundreds of them.

The Carrion is dark indeed.

If Q and Cid had somehow managed to find a way to follow us through the stadium room, Ryan might be leaving enough of a trail for them to follow, even though our route is so erratic.

But the thing is, I just can't see how they'd have done it.

We eat a little at night in a dim room, and this time I have absolutely nothing to shit. I try, but the most I can manage are a few drops of piss. The room we sleep in has a low ceiling. It's maybe twenty feet wide or so, and the floor is filled with gravel mounds.

They lay me down between a couple of them.

I see the gravel mound to the right of me has melted halfway into the floor. The one to my left is hollow. Inside I see movement.

Jesus.

A corpse.

With one rotten eye and one empty socket, it stares at me through the thin cage of gravel.

"There's a corpse in this mound," I warn.

Durgan shrugs.

"I don't like sleeping next to the dead," I say.

"I'm dead," the wight responds.

"I don't like sleeping next to you either."

Durgan doesn't sleep, and come to think of it, I don't think I've ever seen him sleep. He stands watch at the doorway. A wight can be a damn useful thing.

And I think of my son, of how things could have been between us.

Ryan is shivering, and his movement bothers me.

I close my eyes, but the fact that the corpse is staring at me makes it nearly impossible to sleep. Maybe I'll sleep on Durgan's back tomorrow.

I hear some shifting, and I jerk awake.

The corpse is still stuck.

From where I lay tied, I roll over onto my numb hands and look to my right. There Ryan is, shivering in the corner. His right arm is flaking too. I hadn't noticed that, but the fireball which gave his face that faux-sunburn must have gotten him there as well. Unless—

He's rubbing his hand, peeling off dead skin. Pieces

fall like a rain of connected dandruff. His fingernail comes off with one chunk of the crusty shedding flesh and falls to the floor by his feet.

Okay. That's not a burn.

Ryan's shaking alright, not from the cold Carrion air, but from pain. He turns to me, perhaps aware that I can see him. His face is loose, almost like it's melting off and, I see the beginnings of the healing beneath it—a pale skin, the kind of skin that has never seen even the dim light of these caverns.

"Durgan," I say softly.

"I'm aware, Godslayer."

"Did he swallow corpsedust?"

Durgan, still maintaining his watch, shakes his head. "He's not rotting."

"What then?"

"I don't know."

"Should we kill him?" I ask.

"Probably," he answers, but makes no move to do so.

Ryan shakes some more but then does something even more terrible. He looks at me calmly, and becomes completely relaxed. "The men of the Carrion bury their dead under even mounds of stone," he says. "We must be near a tribe, for the stones they use are mined from their quarries. If the body becomes ambulatory during its somnolence, the hellstone, as it heals, purifies the corpse, taking it piece by piece, atom by precious atom, with it into the stone."

And then he goes back to shaking.

Fuck me. Something is so severely wrong with that dude that I don't even know what to say. Does he have some kind of walking stilling? Still men can waste away, but I've not heard of them shedding their damn skin.

Is there some kind of hellacious parasite that burrows into a man?

None that I've ever heard of, but Hell is vast and full of strange evils.

I resign myself to a night of wakefulness.

The cool stone seeps into my ankle, and I thought that might make me feel better, but instead, the new flavor of pain is more distracting. But hey, it's not like I was going to be sleeping anyways.

The corpse struggles against its gravel. I see the stone has healed into its body. In a few years, maybe decades, it would heal the whole corpse away, if Ryan is right.

"I feel you, brother," I whisper to the corpse. "I feel you."

I can't explain it, but I awaken fresh and alert. I may have slept for an hour, tops—and it can't have been good sleep because my God damned ankle feels like the armies of Mordor strolled over it last night—but shit all if I care how I got this way.

How do we take Hell? One day at a time.

Let me tell you a secret. I think I can walk today. My ankle is horrific, but I bet after a few minutes, it would limber up. I'm sure as hell not telling anybody though.

I turn to the corpse beside me. For all I know, it's been staring at me the entire night.

"I love you too, sweetheart," I tell it.

Fin's shadow covers me. "You sick motherfucker, flirting with a corpse."

I shrug. "He wants me."

With a careful motion, I roll up to my knees, holding my hands back so that Fin can untie and retie them in front of me . . . but I feel sly. Before, I'd laid my wrists flat against each other when they tied me up. Not this time. This time I blade one wrist.

Keith, though he'd watched Fin the first two times he tied me up, apparently now trusts the guy's knots. Honestly, they've been pretty darn tight. I'm sort of amazed my hands haven't fallen off. Had Keith been watching me now, though, I'm sure he would have caught my little bit of deception.

Fin, bless his cancerous little hyena heart, doesn't notice shit.

Guess whose hands are getting circulation today? This guy's.

To boot, if I struggle, I should be able to get my wrists free. A little bit of a distraction and I might even get to test my theories on strangling wights.

I give Durgan a seductive look as Fin steps away from me. "Hey, sweetie. You ready to spend the day with me?"

Durgan's black eyes betray no emotion, but I like to think I frustrate him.

The hyenas are in bad shape, of course. They're under a lot of pressure, Soulfall has soulfucked them, and they've got another day of Carrion marching ahead. Then, to put the whipped cream on the fabulous milkshake that is today, they have to barter me for a favor and something to do with an Angel, and though Keith likes Igraine, I get the feeling that the woman makes the rest of them nervous.

That all makes sense. It's my sanity I'm questioning.

Or should I? It's not like it can get a whole lot worse for me, so maybe I should be looking forward to a change in masters.

Durgan bends down and brings me back up into his fireman's carry. The ceiling is low enough that the tatters of the back of my shirt brush up against it.

The cancer men look at us.

"Onward faithful steed!" I say.

If it takes two people to make a joke, I didn't tell one, but honestly, I'm the only dude here I want to impress—well, and the corpse.

The corpse's rock pile is still as Durgan carries me out of the room.

I'll miss you, sweetie!

I ride my mania and my wight mount through the halls. In the back of my mind, I remember having this kind of glee before—after I'd been diagnosed with cancer in the old world. It had come after a deep depression, a sort of childlike delight at life, a denial that eventually peeled away to reveal how poorly a mind God had designed for men. I crumbled. They said I was dying with grace, but only because the rose-colored glasses of the living are themselves tinted with denial. I must die well, or my parents, my friends, and that one Christian bitch who tasked me with Myla, wouldn't be able to handle my death.

Why? I don't know why. I just know.

Maybe it's because they were going to die too, and they'd need that death to be met with dignity as well.

The Carrion is deadly, dark and deep, its twisted caves and arches giving new meaning to the hyenas' paranoia. For once, I feel a strange kinship with the work of the Architect. The twisted stone pillars which rise and fall from the ceilings as stalagmites and stalactites, the devils near enough that we can hear their breath but who are never close enough to see, the dark rooms and distant cubbies whose light promises darting shadows of both friend and foe, they are all arrayed against Keith's group.

And so am I.

In Maylay Beighlay I'd led Durgan and his men back into the slums to face a pack of rabid half-rotten children. I'd used the chaos Xyn had created against him. This is what it means to be an infidel. Hell is sometimes an opponent, but sometimes it's just home.

What am I, then, if I can call the Carrion my home?

As Durgan scouts the halls ahead, he is forced to

put me down again from time to time.

"I hate this route," Harris mutters while we await Durgan's return.

"Even Igraine's people use this pass," Keith replies softly. "There's not a better way through the Carrion."

"Yes there is," Ryan says, but no one listens.

Durgan returns and leads us onward. The devils slow our progress, but I don't mind. What have the dead but time?

I hear the rushing of either a waterfall or some rapids. I'm sure it's a branch of the Lethe as I've been told that river dominates much of the Carrion. The stone around us seems different somehow. Darker. Colder. Maybe the condensation of the nearby source of water keeps the area even colder than the rest of this damn region.

Flecks of colorless crystal are embedded in the worked-stone walls here, and the brilliant glimmers of their reflected light seem like a star-filled night sky. A set of stairs hides in the shadows of our room, and one by one, Keith and his men disappear down the steps.

For whatever reason, Durgan and I go last.

The sound of the waterfall is deafening as we enter the next room.

A light blue skystone vein snakes its way through the high natural ceiling, providing only enough light to keep the cavern from being completely dark. The nearly black rock here is entirely unworked, and were it not for the unusual light of the skystone, I could have mistaken it for an old world cave.

Water tumbles through the ceiling along the back wall in a wide stream which is perhaps seventy feet across and fifty feet tall. The velocity of its waters is sufficient to make me think the fall must have descended for at least another two-hundred feet before it enters this chamber. Its rolling descent is made uneven by brave, sharp boulders which jut out from the wall of whitecapped water. The waters form a lake of sorts, with islands of stalagmites rising out from its surface.

"Watch out for the whirlpools," Durgan shouts above the deafening roar. "Much of the water escapes this chamber through cracks in the whetstone floor. The suction at times can be enough to rip out your intestines."

The hyenas nod quietly.

They haven't been here before, I realize, otherwise Durgan would have no need to warn them. So was Keith Igraine's bitch before he joined the Order, then? Or maybe everyone just used a different entrance?

A million and one questions.

We make our way over the uneven stone. In places, the current picks up and is quite strong, but as we move along the left edge of the room, we come to a portion of the lake which is nearly still.

Durgan is the first to enter.

My feet are the second, and the water is so unbelievably cold that the toes on my good foot curl inside Jessica's boot. As we continue, the water rises to Durgan's shoulders. Since he's got me in a fireman's carry, I have to arch my back and lift my head to breathe. Fortunately, the buoyancy of the water makes that easier than I'd expect.

The hyenas fan out around us, and I see them steering clear of the patches of current, heeding the warning Durgan had given earlier.

We approach the wall of water.

"No sudden movements!" Keith calls out over the rush. "They've spotted us."

"Let's hope there hasn't been a coup," Harris yells back. "Maab wants your head, you know. They could shoot us all down right now."

"I don't even know these motherfuckers!" I yell to whomever might be watching.

None of Keith's cancer men has a sense of humor, but maybe, if I can be heard over the waterfall, one of the men supposedly watching us does.

"Don't worry," Keith calls back to Harris. "She still has to deal with Lucreas Crassus. As long as they need him, we're good."

It'd be neat if he was wrong, but then again, I might get hit in the crossfire. And what an ironic way to die that would be.

A light, perhaps from a flashlight, shines out from behind the waterfall where I expected there to be only stone.

"This way!" Keith shouts.

We slog up to the fall. The force of it is tremendous on my back as Durgan and I become completely submerged. My ankle isn't taking this well.

The wight's muscles power us upward.

Then the water gives way and we're in a dim corridor. I sputter and cough until my breathing evens out.

Shotguns are pointed at us, wielded by darkly dressed men. They look different from the Order in that the weave of their grey fabric is looser, though their faces are just as cruel.

I wonder if they know their shot and slugs won't hurt Durgan.

One by one, the hyenas crawl in from the waterfall. Unlike Durgan, it is a supreme effort for them, and like me, they sputter and cough.

Not Keith though, he arrives gracefully, cutting through the water to stand with us. "I've brought Igraine a present," he says, pointing to me.

"Wait here," one man says. "I'll check with a priestess."

The priestess is a slender blonde woman with the apparent disposition of a corporate raider. She has a strong widow's peak, with her long, straight hair pulled back into a ponytail. It reminds me of Cid. At her side is what one of the men addresses as a "Little Lady." The Little Lady is around four and a half feet tall and probably somewhere between seven and nine years old.

Durgan has laid me on the side of the cavern, and the priestess gives me a once over before turning back to Keith. "You can't seriously expect me to believe that's Cris."

In the dull light, I can't tell if her eyes are blue or green.

I spent three years trying to track down Myla. Without Q's help, I probably wouldn't have been able to catch her. However, I wonder if maybe he knew she went to the Carrion and didn't tell me. It's possible. If so, it probably saved my life.

I kind of doubt it, though. Q was always a swim-at-your-own-risk kind of guy.

Keith smiles. "It's Cris. It definitely is."

"I can vouch for this," Durgan's voice rumbles.

"He's an infidel, too!" Fin pipes up, impressing no one.

The priestess' cold eyes return to me. "Igraine will be able to smell a rat. Her and Myla spent two nights together when Xyn was here."

Slut.

Keith spreads his arms. "It's him. I'm telling you, he'll get you to Blood Pass."

"I still don't believe you," she says in an annoyed tone, "but I see no choice but to let you have an audience." She nods toward Ryan. "You need to leave your leper here. Is he in withdrawal?"

The swim through the waterfall hadn't done Ryan any favors. His skin is a mottled patchwork of alabaster white and corpse-like grey. A leper he's not, but I have *no* problem leaving him behind.

She's right about the withdrawal, though, that dude is shaking. Maybe he'd taken something in Soulfall, something like corpsedust or wightdust that I just hadn't heard of, and he's suffering its absence now.

His face, a mask of terror, calms in that weird way of his. "I will wait here on the while."

That dude is *gone*.

Durgan hoists me over his shoulders again and Ryan takes my spot against the cool stone.

"If you say any of that 'onward faithful steed' bullshit," Keith says to me sternly, "I swear to God I will blow your brains out, Angel be damned."

The Little Lady begins snickering. From where I'm slung over Durgan's shoulder, I give her a wink.

As a response she mimes sucking a dick by opening her mouth, moving her fist back and forth, and sticking one tongue against her cheek.

The idea of someone so young doing something so sexual makes me want to retch.

She finds my reaction just as funny as Keith's

retelling of my joke.

Well, these guys work with the Order. I can't expect them to be good people. Still, though, that shit is just wrong.

The priestess leads us down a tunnel that has been worked over by clay bricks. While not up to the standards of the ancients, Igraine's people were miles ahead of even the masons in Maylay Beighlay.

A single indention runs along the right hand side of the tunnel at about head height. I've no idea what it's for, but it's too small to be a shelf. Maybe they put bullets there or something?

Other parts of the tunnel's construction make more sense. We pass by wooden pillars which support large flagstones in the roof. My assumption is that if you knocked the pillars down, the tunnel would collapse.

Everyone in Hell knows that holing up is a bad idea, that Minotaurs relish finding those places, so I'm guessing this must be a defense for that—but attacks can't happen too regularly, or these guys would all be dead.

When the tunnel ends, which Durgan punctuates by knocking my head into the exit archway, we emerge into a place that's quite beautiful.

This stuff was *definitely* built by the ancients.

The floors are made of polished marble and granite. The marble is laid out like tile, forming smooth paths which run across the enormous chamber. Outside of the paths, the shiny granite stones are fitted together like some sort of giant jigsaw puzzle. The patterns their cracks make in the floor seem haphazard when I look directly at one spot, but their irregularities form geometric shapes when I give the ground a broader glance. Pillars, appearing almost Arabic in the way their bell-like shapes sweep up to the forty foot ceiling, stand decoratively, lining the marble paths, their regular slender forms doing little to obstruct my view of the chamber. Near the base of each pillar, a tiny alcove had been carved out, and inside each one stands a heroic classical-styled figure.

A squat central pillar, made in a pseudo-Doric style, is obscenely large—perhaps eighty feet in diameter. Unfortunately, some asshole—and I'm betting they're the current resident—had a gigantic tunnel carved right into the middle of that pillar. They'd done some good work with the arch above it, showing the figure of a man who is slitting the throat of a bull, but the effect of it is, on the whole, somewhat disturbing.

Steps, carved just a little unevenly, lead down into the breached pillar.

And who would have guessed, that's where they're taking us.

As we pass more life-sized statues, I whisper into Durgan's ear, "I bet you'd be fucking awesome at playing hide-and-go-seek in here."

As always, he pays me no mind, but I'm convinced it's a front.

"Or, if that's not your game," I drone on, "maybe a little Ollie-Ollie-Oxen-Free?"

And for one beautiful moment, his boot scuffs the marble floor. He catches his balance almost perfectly, hardly missing a stride, but I'd done it. I'd opened up a crack in his seemingly invincible suit of emotional armor.

Give me enough time and I'll quarry down to his heart.

I'm not sure if he'd taken much physical damage when I'd left him alone in the rotten streets of Maylay Beighlay, but I bet you he at least lost most of his men. God knows I don't see any of them here.

Down the steps we go.

And down.

And down.

Christ Jesus, this place is deep.

From time to time we pass by landings, and I see into shadow-filled tunnels where men work at the stone. Here and there I see collapses, which makes me think these people must be very brave, or very stupid, or most likely, very desperate.

Whatever they're using the stone for must be something damn important or else they wouldn't risk destabilizing their environment, right?

The stairs bottom out into a grey room which is lit

by burning woodstone torches.

Serious guards, well armed, well fed and well muscled, stop us.

Our priestess speaks up. "No weapons in the pit. You'll all be stripped and cavity searched."

Even her men hand over their weapons, which surprises me.

Fuck, they're going to have to untie me to get my shirt off, and I'm not sure if I can get away with blading my wrist a second time.

As a guard steps up to me, I meet his steely gaze. "Bend me over, big boy," I tell him.

The Little Lady giggles. "I like him, Sasha," she tells our priestess.

"You might be able to have him," Sasha responds, "*if* you finish your studies, and *if* he's alive when Igraine is through with him."

For some reason, this infuriates my guard.

"Easy with my ankle," I warn him.

He does no such thing, and is extraordinarily rough in tugging my pants off my wounded leg. The pain brings tears to my eyes—but that gives me an idea.

"And with the shirt, too," I say. "It's pretty tattered, I wouldn't want it to get ripped any."

Obligingly, he rips my shirt off.

Well ain't you just the brightest little knife in the cowshed. Now they aren't going to have to retie my hands, so I get to keep my good circulation.

Of course, as I see even Durgan bend over in the nude to accept a cavity search, I realize my guard is going to have the last laugh.

We descend into the pit via a long circular staircase. One wall along the stairs is crystal, so as Durgan carries my ass down, I can see a hazy and distorted view of the room we're entering. It's large, certainly, and it looks like it has cages honeycombed along its circular walls. As fucked up as this place must be to have raised this hellion they call the Little Lady, I've got to give Igraine credit for keeping so many people alive in the Carrion. I mean, sure, most of them are slaves, and that can't be the most effective way to organize a workforce, but from a numbers standpoint, it surely is impressive.

I wonder if any of the slaves are philosophical enough to thank their lucky stars they aren't at the maw of a hound every morning. I doubt it because I wouldn't be either. I'd rather the demons than the cage, I think.

I think.

The spiral stairway bottoms out onto the pit floor, and I get a better view of the room as Durgan carries me out. There is a landing, perhaps half the size of a football field, filled with darkly-dressed Carrion soldiers. They clump together, speaking quietly amongst themselves. Are these the Carrion born Keith had alluded to earlier? None of them, of course, have any weapons, but their uniforms are well made.

Rising upward and outward from the floor of the pit are the same kinds of arches I saw in the stadium chamber, except this time the steps are far steeper. Each tier is perhaps twelve feet above the next, but their landings are only a foot wide or so. Each arched room is about ten feet deep, and covered at the front with a set of iron bars. Each set of bars has a locked door and a prisoner. The prisoners cling to the bars and look down at us with a sort of sadistic voyeurism which bothers me. These were the cages I'd thought were hexagonal when looking through the crystal.

I look up to see where the cages end, but after a quarter of a mile or so they disappear into the darkness. Somewhere above that must loom our distant ceiling.

A din fills the chamber as the prisoners begin speaking, I assume to each other, and I assume about us.

On the far side of the pit, the perfect circle of cages is interrupted by a huge stage which appears Mayan in the way each step is its own level. Like all of the stone in this deep cavern, the stage is carved out of the same deep and dark grey hellstone that the mines above were quarried from. On the wall behind the stage is a tremendous tapestry made of red cloth. And when I say tremendous, I mean it. It's perhaps forty yards wide and thirty yards tall, and a golden man is emblazoned upon it, straddling a tremendous golden bull while yanking its head back by the horns, his golden dagger drawing golden blood from the beast's golden throat.

In front of that tapestry is a polished, black marble throne, its lavender and vermillion veins matching its crimson embroidered purple cushions. The crowd of soldiers parts for us as Keith and the priestess lead us to the throne.

The woman on the throne is as elegant a creature as I have seen in either of the worlds I have lived in. Her lightly tanned limbs—the devil knows what she did to get that tan—are long, shapely, and graceful. Her smooth-shaven calves reflect the light of the burning braziers which flank the stage.

Chained about her are two dozen naked men, and I can see she clearly has a type. She likes well-muscled slaves with dark hair and light eyes—men like Keith. There are a few blondes, an Asian of some flavor, a black man and two Hispanic fellows, but other than that, they are all Clark Kent looking motherfuckers.

Other soldiers, their dark shirts lined with purple, stand guard around her throne. With no weapons here, the ability to fight with fists must be at a premium. I'm guessing these are her best fighters. An interesting strategy to survive in a kingdom where you mistreat all your subjects to the point where they'd shoot you.

There could be another explanation. They had mentioned a person named Maab was capable of performing a coup. Maybe someone is stirring up undue resentment, and this weaponless hole is her justified reaction.

Maybe.

But looking at the broken-souled hunks which line her stage . . . and oh God, has she even broken their . . . that bitch. At least half of them have suffered some kind of damage to their genitals.

Keith is becoming a more and more attractive captor every damn second.

Movement beneath the twenty foot raised stage catches my attention. There is a larger cage beneath her, and in it I see only blackness thanks to the angle of the braziers on her stage—but there is something moving down there.

I catch sight of the head of a bull and the torso of a man.

"Keith," I say from Durgan's back as the wight's even gait rocks me back and forth, "is there a Minotaur below that stage?"

Keith does not turn around, but his head nods.

Dear fucking God.

Above Igraine, hanging in a gilt cage to stage left, is a woman. Not a woman.

Oh no. Not a woman.

She too is slender and elegant, but so much more slender than a human should be. Her skin is bleached with sorrow, and her tear-touched eyes are wide, innocent, and tortured. White-feathered wings emerge from her shoulders before sweeping around her cage and ending with their tips nearly touching in front of her feet. A few of her feathers seem too short, as if they were sheared off—and of course they were, because Igraine wouldn't want an Angel who could fly. That bitch had clipped the Angel's wings.

Her face is a wonder to behold, just alien enough to be exotic, just Caucasian enough to be familiar, and just holy enough to break my heart.

I realize now that Igraine is as dangerous and as powerful as Xyn, and judging from the prisoners she keeps, twice as evil.

We stop before the stage. A silence envelops us as Igraine shifts slightly in her chair. I can hear the snorting of the Minotaur now that the din has died away.

This woman has captured an Angel and a Minotaur. A devil is beneath her, an Angel above her, and she sits between them, the ruler of all that she sees.

But I have to focus. I tear my eyes away from Igraine and the Angel and the Minotaur and look at the others on the stage. There is a man dressed in a grey-skin armor, except the color of the grey gives way to purple now and again as the light shifts on it. He is broad, and his face is full of a self-assured cruelty I don't quite know how to describe. Behind him, kneeling, are a few gaunt-faced slaves dressed in light brown robes. They look particularly malnourished, gaunt shoulders and bony knees jutting up under the drab fabric.

I look back up to the cage and see that the Angel's eyes are on me. Her sadness is existential and brutal to behold. That sort of malaise should never strike a creature so pure. I try to smile at her, but I too am in pain. I too am injured.

And then with horror I see she has a swollen belly.

Please tell me, oh God, if you can hear me, please tell me she is not pregnant. Please.

Igraine probably had her raped just to see what would come out.

The priestess steps forward and speaks. "Lady Igraine, though I personally do not think it likely, your asset Keith has brought us a man he claims is Cris."

Igraine's eyes narrow for a brief moment.

"The boyfriend of Myla, my Queen," the Little Lady clarifies. "The one who might know how to get to

Blood Pass."

Igraine's brilliant blue eyes find me, and her thin pink lips part just slightly.

"I'd bow to you, my Queen," I say, and then Durgan drops me unceremoniously to the floor, "but I just got body slammed by a wight."

"Rise," her clear voice orders.

Who am I to disobey?

I stand as best I can on one foot, and then gingerly lean just a smidgen of weight onto my wounded ankle.

Yup, still hurts, but I bet it would bear my weight if I asked it to.

I'm not going to ask, though.

Balancing on one foot with your hands tied is no easy thing, but I try.

"Step forward, Keith," she says.

I have to look up to see the faces of the slaves in their cages. They are so quiet, it's hard to imagine they're there. I can hear the Angel sadly weeping, and the Minotaur's short snorts, but from the men in the cages, I hear nothing.

Keith takes two steps toward the stage.

The eyes of the cruel man behind the throne bear into my current captor. Jealousy, perhaps? Something I can use? Maybe, or maybe it's just the attention of a professional bodyguard.

"Keith," she says, rolling his name across her tongue like a dark chocolate truffle, "Keith, Keith, Keith.

My prodigal son. You always bring me such strange gifts."

Keith bows his head for a second. "My Queen, I do not deserve your for—"

"You do not," she says.

His head jerks back up as if he'd been struck. "I know you think Lucreas Crassus has returned to the City of Blood and Stone. I know you wish you had a way to spy on him."

There are grunts amongst the slaves, but none of surprise.

Igraine's face is slightly amused. "You've a fertile mind, but I might be interested in finding Blood Pass, yes."

I realize this is actually happening. They're going to make me show them the way back to the City of Blood and Stone. Good God. I *might* be able to backtrack. Maybe the rooms would jog my memory, but I feel a clenching in my heart as I remember the oppressive mines and the angry black-eyed dyitzu who beat us until we gave every ounce of energy our bodies and souls could muster. And I remember the ones with red eyes, and the hounds at the Minotaur's beck and call. And I remember the six-armed monstrosity that flew above the ravines at night.

It's where I found Myla.

I can't go back there.

Not now.

Not ever.

I'd rather die.

If I see one of those places along the way, where Ares dragged us to safety, maybe that place where Myla and I held hands under the light of the crystal while Q stood guard . . . I'd . . . I'd . . .

Myla, I miss you.

Why? Why'd you have to take our son?

They're talking and I need to pay attention. How could I be so stupid as to miss this—

"That's quite a bargain." Igraine's voice is slightly amused. "What would you ask the Angel about?"

Keith looks up at the lovely caged creature. "I need to ask her about God."

Igraine's amusement grows. "She's never met him, nor met any Angel who has, but if you want to know about God, Keith, all you need do is ask me."

Keith nods. "Of course, my Queen. I don't want to ask for myself. I am doing the work of the Order here."

She leans back from her crossed legs and bounces her top foot. I notice for the first time her golden high heeled shoes and am struck by how attractive the lacing, which comes up the first half of her calf, makes her look.

"What do I care of the Order," she says, and her face goes into a mock pout, "except that they stole you away from me?"

And then there is a ruckus from the slaves above.

They are laughing, laughing with their queen. They're laughing at Keith.

Those fucked up people, they're identifying with their captor. They're enjoying watching her do in miniature the damage which she has so massively done to them.

Keith shrinks from her, but then regains his backbone. "I cannot speak for you, my Queen, but I wouldn't guess you cared about the Order at all. I thought you cared about Blood Pass. That's the reason why I brought you this man."

He motions to me.

Igraine's eyes again find me. "Do you know the way to Blood Pass?"

I shrug, as honest an answer as I know, and the intake of breath from the surrounding cages, and the horrid look of empathy coming from the Angel tells me my response had better be a specific one.

"I have traveled it, Queen," I say. "It is my belief that I can find it again, given a little time."

She leans forward. "If you are Cris," her thin lips smile, "and you told me with surety you knew the way, I'd know you were lying. But are you Cris?"

"I am. No 'h' to avoid confusion."

Her smile widens, and I see her perfectly white teeth. "Prove to me that you are the man who Myla once loved."

My heart beats in the sense of quiet expectation

hanging in the room. Again I look to the cage, and there is my Angel, looking at me, her eyes supportive. She believes me.

But how can I prove this to Igraine? Wait, they spent two nights together. Was it really sexual? Was Xyn there?

"He is, I can verify," Durgan says. "He killed my master."

Igraine sneers and shakes her head. "Your words are worthless to me, wight." She returns her attention to me. "Cris, I asked you a question."

I raise my chin and speak up loudly. "Myla had inverted nipples. And for the first few days of Aiden's life . . ." I have to pause to avoid crying, "his jaw was slightly offset. He could not suckle. We had no pumps or anything, so I drew the milk into my mouth and put it into his."

Igraine stretches, and I see the pull of the black fabric across her modest breasts. "I do believe you are Cris."

I almost sigh in relief. This is my moment. I need to get out from under Keith's thumb. Is Igraine worse than he is? Probably, but I have to try to play some cards here.

"There are things I need to tell you," I say. "Things I cannot share in public. I need to meet with you privately."

Igraine becomes truly amused now, and Keith's

head jerks toward me.

"He's an infidel!" Keith warns. "He escaped from Xyn's prison when everyone thought he was beaten beyond the ability to move. Then he came back and killed Xyn."

Igraine gives her pouty-frown-face again for a half second. "He was no Infidel Friend when he was with Myla."

"He is dangerous," Keith says. "If you alone must hear him, rupture a guard's eardrums."

Durgan steps forward again. "It is known that when the infidels sense an Archdevil encroaching upon their territory, they call their men out. Then they send in someone like Endymion, or one of the Kin to slay the Archdevil. This is what happened in Maylay Beighlay, and Cris is the one who came. I do not know how he escaped from our cell, but I would consider him incredibly dangerous. I would not recommend you be alone in the same room as he."

Durgan stops, surely realizing he just played right into my hands.

"La'Ferve," Igraine's voice is like honey. "Take the Order to a cell. And please, have someone prepare my home chamber. I want to speak with the . . . infidel," and she laughs, "alone."

XIV

Guards, dressed in black with purple trim, flank me as I painfully limp my way through the halls behind Igraine's stage. I'm not sure where she went, but she left shortly before I was taken away. The four of them stay close but do not put their hands on me. As we pass other slaves and soldiers, I do my best to pretend these guards are an escort, not a prison detail.

I'm unsure if it helps.

The halls themselves are Carrionesque. The black hellstone is interrupted by deep purple bricks. In this inner sanctum, all of the stone faces have been polished. I see a dark reflection of myself limping alongside me.

Hang tough there, little reflection. I'll see what I

can do to get us out of this.

The people we pass in the halls are almost always robed women, priestesses of some kind or another, and quite a few of them are Little Ladies. There are men walking around as well, but they're not the soldier type. I believe they're a flavor of slave—but are well fed, oiled, and almost always nude. When they're wearing anything at all, it's usually some sort of jewelry, or boots, or wrist brace—something to highlight their nudity rather than cover it.

Torchlight shines out from behind a bend in the corridor before us, and when we take the turn, I see a silver double door. The right one's ajar.

"You may enter," one of the guards says.

My heart goes apeshit in my chest. I reach out and grab one of the silver handles, brace myself on my good foot, and pull. It opens easily on greased hinges.

I behold Igraine's chamber.

For Igraine, I realize, some of the old world rules still apply. You could tell a lot about a woman from her room back up there. In Hell, a girl's home is mostly a thing of necessity, but when she has this much power, I've no doubt her chambers say a good bit about her.

The floor is covered by hound hides, their even cut and brushed fur giving me the impression of carpet. The hounds they'd chosen were black with red fringes, and the arrangement makes the accented colors look like veins in marble. The left wall, save for a squared off extension, is made of either ironglass or steelglass. Behind it, water, lit up with blue and purple hues, gently flows.

This is one of the light sources of the room.

The other is the right wall, beyond which seems to flow a slow river of molten lava. That would mean it had to be steelglass or something even stronger. It couldn't be lava, could it? It must be some sort of illusion.

But nonetheless, heat radiates from the right wall, while cold air comes from the left. The differences in temperature are not unpleasant, and the mixed lighting means that all the furniture and statues in the room are colored in both cool and hot tones.

The furniture has almost certainly been cannibalized from the ancients. Divans, a few lounge chairs and couches make separate blocks where people might come to sit and talk in groups. Some seats, and what might have been an early version of a futon, surround a dinner table. The arms of the chairs are often carved into the faces of men, or gods, or mythological beasts. The embroidery on the seat backs and cushions are almost always gold, and are filled with flowers, and trees, and strangely, some have spiderwebs. Cupboards, their doors inlaid with glass so I can see the fine dishes beyond, line some of the walls.

In the extension on the left wall, I see her bed. It's a four poster, a fully-canopied Emperor-sized mattress with old world sheets.

At one table sits Igraine.

She is perhaps even more striking up close. Her blonde hair smoothly drapes across one shoulder, tumbling down her back in a series of loose curls. Not one of those hairs is out of place.

Her arms are completely feminine, long, and graceful—smooth enough to hide any cut of muscle, but shapely enough to be devoid of any excess fat. Adorning her is the same black and purple dress she wore on the throne. She's simultaneously both at ease and holding herself with perfect posture, one long smooth leg crossed over the other. Again I find the sandal-like ties, which rise from her high heels and snake around her shapely calf, strangely seductive.

She's wearing makeup, I believe, because her eyelashes are probably too long and too dark to be natural. Her lips, their color deepened by the light of the magma, are a deep red and her blue eyes belie a great intelligence.

"You may close the door behind you," her high, supremely confident voice intones.

I do as she suggests, happy to put a closed door between myself and the guards.

On the table before her, just inches away from her manicured fingernails, lies a pistol.

With a parsimonious yet supple gesture, she motions to the room around me, perhaps giving me permission to take the rest of it in.

The statues here suit my neoclassical aesthetic and are either renaissance or were carved by the ancients. At first I think they must be later sculptings, not just because of the preternatural skill, but because the women are slender and muscular. In the old world, the Greeks and Romans generally preferred a less fit feminine body type. But I begin to suspect Hell changed what they wanted in a woman. You see, the renaissance artists tended not to be very athletic, so when they sculpted men standing in contrapposto, their subjects seemed off balance. But the Greeks, and the Romans after them, had no such trouble. I think they understood the position as a modified fighting stance, but whatever it was, their subjects didn't look like they were going to tip the fuck over.

The skill here is truly extraordinary, and I almost jump when I see a face I recognize. One of these men has been carved to look like Ares. And, in the odd way that the Romans would, he was made to look like the *God* Ares, his shield crested with a vulture and a hound.

Then I see the Infidel's statue.

I had seen him once in Soulfall, or at least a reflection of him, but this one is so much more real. The man who carved this piece of art, I realize, must have been looking into the actual Infidel's eyes.

The Infidel is the most beautiful man I have ever seen. His face the most human. His hair short and unstyled. About his shoulders hangs the carved representation of robes—but I stop looking as I'm caught by the statue's eyes. Devoid of color, as is the rest of his marble visage, I nonetheless sense there is something unimaginably powerful behind them. Unlike old world statues, the individual details of the man's iris had been represented here in the grey on grey stone. Maybe it's the limit of the abilities of the sculptor which leaves the nature of the Infidel's emotion opaque to me. Maybe. But this much I can tell, whatever the infidel was thinking, however he was feeling, it was . . . world changing. Mind boggling. An epiphany of a sort. Of the sort I'd once felt from Cid and Q.

There's a similarity between all the Infidel Friend, and I'm beginning to realize it doesn't stem so much from their culture as it does from this man. It is his likeness in some way stamped onto their minds, or their moralities, or their bodies.

And in a way, it's the part of them I admire the most. The strength. The capability. The compassion. But there is something else they carry. A willingness to coldly turn their backs on what might be our greater calling. But does that stem from him? Or is that something the desperation of Hell implants upon survivors?

Igraine's voice reaches my ears from where she sits behind me. "It must be a terrible burden for you infidels, to worship a man in place of a god."

And I think about this. Is it?

Surely, as a person, he must have some biases or weaknesses. He must have at some point acted with caprice. A god with human failings would be a terrible thing indeed . . . but then again, I'd never heard of a god who didn't have human failings.

I'd asked to be alone with her for a reason. This is it. I've got to play my bluff, my gambit, because it's my only chance.

"Is it?" I ask without turning around. "He answers more prayers than most gods."

Because I'd bladed my wrist when Fin tied me, I should be able to slip my hand out. I became aware of the trick from working with an illusionist on Earth, but I can't remember how I'm supposed to get my wrist free. Is it thumb first? No, that didn't work. I try to keep my motions small so she doesn't know what I'm doing. Pinky first. Nope. Thumb? Pinky? Each attempt slides my hand farther out. Got it.

I drop the ropes to the ground at my feet as I turn. Then, steeling myself with the strength of the stone man behind me, I take my first step toward her. My ankle explodes with pain, wanting to give way, but I won't let it. Each step is agony, but the sudden narrowing of her eyes as she sees me, unbound and walking unwounded, makes the excruciation worth bearing.

I sit down at the table across from her.

"Keith doesn't know why I've come," I tell her,

"and it's very important that you listen to me extremely carefully."

Her composure isn't really lost, but she's frozen, a tableau of elegance instead of its living, moving embodiment. Then, after a few long seconds pass, she puts her hand on the gun and spins it on the table.

"Okay," she says, "Cris with no 'h.' You've got my attention."

XV

Cid had perfect posture, but Q didn't always, instead sometimes carrying himself in a languid and relaxed manner. Ares, I remember him having, well, both at the same time, which probably isn't possible. Given the choices on offer, I opt to emulate Q. First, he was the guy who trained me, after all, and secondly, it's not like I had enough energy to go all Emily Post on this bitch. I lean back into my seat and do my best to exude confidence.

My ankle is shouting, *"What the fuck did you just do that for?"* he must be saying. *"There was no reason to walk on me like that."*

He's very shortsighted, my ankle.

I hear a perfunctory double knock on her door.

She raises her chin just slightly. "Enter."

A gorgeous man steps into the room. Like the statues here, he's slender, and I can see he's got a good build. It is, however, an odd kind of muscle definition. His body still looks smooth and soft. His left side is illuminated in rippling blue, his center purple, and his right in red. In none of those hues do I see much in the way of veins. There is none of the excessive bulk of muscle that comes with body building, nor the harsh cut that comes with functional athletic strength. He's a pretty boy, in the gym for looks and nothing more.

I don't think any of the men she's held in thrall would have had trouble finding pornography gigs in the old world, and this one is no exception. Igraine, it appears, is a size queen.

Blue eyeshadow surrounds his eyes, and his lashes have been darkened with some artificial substance. In his right arm he carries a tray. On it is a decanter of bloodwater, some sinfruit and some bread.

Moments after I see the platter, the smell of the bread hits me.

My stomach ruins the illusion of my infidel demeanor by growling angrily.

Traitor.

The slave walks over, toe touching before heel as if he's some kind of dancer, gracefully placing the tray on the table between us.

"Two glasses, Methadonis," Igraine orders.

He's got zero control of his facial expressions because I can immediately tell he's become perturbed.

"You said we could drink together," he whines.

"I like to indulge you, my sweet, but your Domina has business."

He pouts like a three-year-old and, with about as much passive aggressive clanking as a person can muster, fetches two glasses out of a cupboard and pours us some bloodwater. My cup is noticeably under-filled.

"Now, Meth," she says in a husky and, if I'm reading her right, somewhat aroused voice, "You don't want me to be harsh with you. Treat our guest right."

He glares at me, and reluctantly pours more into my glass. It's just a shade below the level of Igraine's.

"Meth?" she says lightly.

He's stirring at her voice, which is making me slightly uncomfortable, but—no, no it doesn't, because infidels do not care about nudity.

He pours more, and if he's shorted me at all, I cannot tell.

"You are excused," Igraine says.

"But—"

"Do you want another session with Maab?" Igraine asks in a firm tone.

His eyes widen, and his testicles raise quickly at the mention of Maab.

"No, Domina."

"You want to be a good boy, don't you?"

"Yes, Domina."

He leaves in a hurry, closing the door behind him.

Keith's boys had spoken of Maab and mentioned she might lead a coup. This should be a good opportunity for me to play infidel, and while their information might not be accurate, this is all a longshot anyway.

"Maab will try to remove you soon," I say, testing the waters while doing my best to avoid looking at the bread. "You know that, don't you?"

Igraine reaches out and breaks the bread in two. "Do you infidels ever stop? Must you always try to destroy us from the inside?"

She hands one half of the bread to me and then begins to cut up the sinfruit.

My belly gives out a roar.

Okay, stomach, buddy of mine, this is how it's going to work. I'm going to pull a chunk off this bread and eat it as if I'm just barely hungry. Hell, I'm not even hungry at all. I'm just eating this shit to be polite. Got it?

I pull off a chunk and place it in my mouth. I chew it as my stomach continues to commit mutiny. Hey, your life's on the line too, bud.

"We can stop escalating your internal strife," I say, "and in return maybe you could stop keeping slaves."

As poised as ever, she takes a sip of her bloodwater. "I tolerate you infidels because some of you are women," she says. "And because you make the lives of the Order miserable, and I enjoy seeing that. *And* because you often have information. But rest assured, it is only a matter of time before I get angry and send my tribes to expunge you from the Carrion. You're weak here, you know that, don't you? Do you know why?"

Because who the fuck would want to live in the Carrion?

"I'll bite," I say, popping another piece of bread in my mouth, "why?"

My stomach, finally silent, seems to be getting on board with the plan here, and it's about damn time.

"Because your strategy, your thinking, your very way of being is too *masculine.*"

I shrug. "It's sexy, though."

Her face becomes a rictus sneer of disgust. "The opposite. Men are too dumb to know how to face the devils. It's in your damn balls, all that testosterone. You just *have* to go out there and fight the evil *mano a mano.* But that's not the best way to live in damnation. You must bend rather than stand firm. You must never face the devils directly. You have to let them wash around you, and not touch you. You must hide and furtively leave your sanctuary only to find food and supplies. This is how you survive in Hell, Cris with no 'h.' No other way will do."

I take a sip of my bloodwater.

Holy fuck it's wine. It's actual fucking wine. This is

terrible. I hate wine, and I'm wasting an entire glass of it. Damnation is literally filled with assholes who enjoy this stuff, and here my good-for-nothing ass is, pretending to like it.

The fire hits my stomach, and our current understanding holds . . . though just barely.

I take another bite of bread to still the fire in my esophagus and the upcoming bitching of my guts.

"You and I are in fundamental disagreement on femininity, then," I say.

"Oh?"

"In my view, the ideal woman doesn't have much use for sex slaves. It's a little bit, uh, rapey."

Her eyes narrow. "Your kind have caused no end of death, and the only way to keep you from murdering others with your own overinflated sense of machismo is to keep you in chains. That's not a duty I take lightly, or even want to perform."

I take a bite of sinfruit, letting the sweet juices roll around in my mouth.

Now I realize why my stomach has been quiet. It's posing me with quite another form of mutiny. I feel pressure building in my abdomen and pressing against my asshole.

I'm deciding this right now, oh stomach of mine, we are not shitting. Infidels do not soil themselves.

"So this what's-his-name, Methadonis, he's free?"

She nods. "He is. He chooses to be this way. Those

men can do as they choose."

"Unless of course, he chooses to be male? Or disobey you?"

She sneers again, but this time sardonically. "You'd stop a person from bringing death down on others, wouldn't you? If Methadonis started acting in that way, I'd indeed be forced to imprison him. You'd do no less, you just don't know what kills people, and what doesn't."

An infidel probably wouldn't lose this argument, but I can't come up with a snappy single point . . . or wait, maybe I can.

"Every job requires different tools, Igraine. Someday you're going to need a hammer, and when you reach for it, all you're going to find are a bunch of wet noodles."

Her blue eyes flash and she gives me an amused smile. "Methadonis is my favorite because he's *never* a wet noodle."

I laugh a bit because it was kind of funny, but mostly because I need to be on good terms with her.

The speed with which her emotions just changed is a little disarming.

"Your information?" she says. "You had something to tell me. If not, this is probably not the right way to wheedle your way into my boudoir."

I nod, and take a bite of bread to buy myself some time.

"Keith and his boys will affirm that they chased me and my team to Soulfall. I'm sure you'll have them interrogated shortly, and you'll hear they thought they were chasing me and my son there. They probably think I was trying to save him, even though my boy was on edge."

Her manicured fingers tap gently on the table. She swirls her wine in a delicate gesture I don't dare try to copy and then sips it.

"So you have them fooled," she says, smiling into her glass as she takes another sip.

"I do."

"And you're going to tell me the truth?" She puts the glass down and then lets her hand rest on the gun.

"I am."

"I'm not a patient woman," Igraine tells me.

You're not really a woman at all. "Why'd you deal with Xyn?" I ask quickly.

She pulls her head back, a motion which would give any normal human woman a double chin, but somehow this bitch has been graced with the most aesthetically calibrated set of genetics I've ever seen.

"He tricked his way in," she admits. "I don't like dealing with demons, but he'd already seen the inside of our complex. He knew our entrances, our exits. And his offers . . ."

I'd struck a nerve here. She really regrets whatever concessions she made to him.

I give her a rueful grin. "He took the woman I love away from me, and my child. Believe me, I know how tricky that son of a bitch could be."

Her blue eyes focus on me, and I can practically feel the whir of her mind. "You killed him?"

"I did."

She takes a sinfruit slice and chews it, leaving her pointer finger on her lips for a moment. "Why did you go to Soulfall?"

That's an excellent question, and there's no avoiding it, so I lay out my lie. "A weapon. The ancients forged it. You know how Archdevils are immune to most substances?"

Her eyes widen in a tiny moment of exasperation. "Of course."

"This weapon is supposed to be able to hurt them all."

She almost chews her lip, but somehow her sense of propriety is enough to save her from performing such an unladylike gesture. "Maybe they forged it to fight Saint Wretch?"

I don't know what the fuck Saint Wretch is, but hey, if it makes sense to her. "Quite possibly. At any rate, the reason we used my son was because we thought he could get by the evil force down there. As a wight, it might not be aligned against him."

She looks at me. "And it didn't work?"

I frown. "It did. But the weapon wasn't there. El

Cid thought it'd been taken to the City of Blood and Stone."

I avoid studying her too closely because, although I'd really like to see if she's gotten a whiff of all the bullshit I'm slinging, I'd rather not give her the opportunity to read me.

"So why are you here?" she asks.

"Keith thinks my team is following him, but he's wrong," I say. "Please don't tell him, but the truth is that my team's dead. I lost my son. It's down to me now. I thought about tricking Keith and his boys into taking me to the City, and then getting them killed there, but Durgan is hard to fool, and Keith's men didn't handle Soulfall well."

Half-truths are best.

She spins the gun and stops it with its barrel pointed right back at me. "But you did handle Soulfall."

"No. No I didn't, but I did better than most."

Again, the half-truths hopefully sound convincing. I meet her eyes and focus on how beautiful they are. How beautiful she is.

If there was just some way to snag a good soul and give it this body.

She spins the gun again, stopping it so the barrel is pointed a little to my left. "I presume you want me to help you get this weapon."

"Yes."

She giggles. "I have no interest in making the

infidels stronger."

She used this tactic with Keith, and he answered by offering her things she did want. I guess, in a way, she runs her place as a sort of Switzerland. Keep your head low, and hope the infidels and the demons all kill each other.

"I imagine not," I say. "And I assume a leader like yourself wouldn't want to overtly piss off the City either."

She uncrosses her legs and sits up straight. "Make your offer." Though I'm taller, her posture seats her higher than me.

"I need a little time to heal my ankle," I say. "Give me a week. Give me a small team. I'll show you Blood Pass in exchange for their help in getting to the City. They'll offer me a modicum of protection."

"You're trying to shortchange me," she playfully accuses. "If you get a weapon like that, it's worth a lot more than Blood Pass. Why don't I kill you and take it myself?"

I shrug. "Might work, but I'm betting you don't have a good way to break into the City. Blood Pass pays for my freedom, and nothing more. If I get the weapon, the infidels will be *very* thankful. We'll kill an Archdevil of your choice."

If she could have sat up any straighter, she would have. I see a shiver run through her body.

"You're offering to clear Londinium," she says, her

voice husky, her cheeks flushed as if she's close to climax.

"I am indeed."

"Would the infidels do that just because you asked them to?" She seems concerned, but I can tell she wants to believe me.

"Doesn't matter," I say in what I hope sounds like a nonchalant tone. "I'm making you that offer. I killed Xyn, remember?"

She looks at the ceiling for a long moment. "I believe you, Cris."

I feel butterflies in my stomach, and my heart leaps with the sudden feel of freedom. I'll heal. I'll get a Carrion team. I'll ditch them and then see if I can find Cid. Sure, finding her would be a ridiculous longshot bordering on a miracle, but . . .

Igraine's asking me something. I listen, all the while doing my best to hide my elation.

" . . . was just a ruse. You had Aiden on edge to get him into Soulfall."

"Correct."

"Your deal is a good one. How can I trust you'll follow through?" I can tell she's already agreed to this, she's just trying to cover all her bases.

"I'm an infidel," I tell her. "I won't promise you something I don't intend to deliver."

She seems to accept this. "You appear unarmed. I can get you some weapons. A Heckler and Kotch, perhaps? That's what you infidels prefer in the Carrion." She smiles, looking like she's about to add in some sarcasm. "And maybe I can get you a suit of purple dyitzu armor, like you saw La'Ferve wearing."

I laugh at that. "Some weapons will be fine. No need to spare your rare dyitzu skins."

She flashes me a knowing grin. "You wouldn't feel more comfortable being shot in purple?"

"Well, at least I'd die pretty," I joke.

She stands up and puts her hands on the table, leaning forward. I can see the hint of her cleavage and, even as starved as I am, as close to shitting myself as I am, as wounded as I am, I can't help but feel a little aroused by her.

"Can I tell you a secret?" she asks.

"Of course."

Her perfect, white teeth shine in the blue light. "You're not an infidel," she whispers.

She points her gun at me in a motion so smooth, there's no real cue for me to react to.

Two men emerge, one from either side of the flowing lava glass wall. They must have been there the whole time, hidden in cubbies behind the illumination.

What had tipped her off? I run through the conversation.

I might still be able to salvage this.

Aiden. She'd said his name. She'd known him. Had I accidently said we'd used wight dust on him? Infidels wouldn't do that. Fuck.

"You're in error," I tell her in what I hope sounds like a calm voice. "I'm in some rather serious pain, and I might have misheard one of your questions—"

Her beautiful head shakes. "Oh no, Cris with no 'h.' No infidel would poison a child with wightdust just to get a weapon, no matter how powerful it was. No infidel would confuse Icanitzu skin armor with dyitzu skin. I know Myla, and you're no Infidel Friend. And, of course, there's the fact that we stripped searched you and found you had no mark. Now what I will believe is that you were on your way to becoming an infidel. You may have even had something to do with scouting in Maylay Beighlay. My people tell me that Q was the one who probably killed Xyn. Q's an unusual choice, so I doubted the report, but you . . . you're far less likely."

She smiles as one of her men grabs me by the armpits and hoists me up.

She walks around the table, her gun held loosely at her side. "Myla did speak of you. She said you were more style than substance. More words than man. That's why she left you, you know. In the end, you're just a trickster. Lies fail when the bullets fly, little man."

Dear God, why did you make women gossip so much? Seriously.

And how is Myla *still* fucking me over? I'm starting to not regret having her murdered by corpses.

As her guards take a firm grip of my arms, she

dares to come close to me. I consider kicking her with my good foot, or hell, even my bad one, but unless I could kill her with a single strike, it wouldn't be worth it.

She reaches forward and puts a condescending hand on my cheek. "Let me tell you your future, little liar. Myla did her best to show me Blood Pass, and failed, but she felt you might have a better shot. I'm going to have some of my people take you there, and you're going to help them find it, to the best of your ability. Then you're going to come back, and assuming you survive all that, I'm going to give you the most terrific and horrifying surprise of your life."

Her hand pats my face a couple of times, and I bite back my anger. "I'll still need to heal."

"No you don't, not really." She looks to one guard. "Take him to a table. Be careful in your kruk selection, though. Not Jeremy. He's apt to kill people. How about Melvin? He should do a lot of damage and still leave Cris alive."

My body is shaking, with fear or anger, or hate, I don't know.

I don't even know what a kruk is, or who these people are, or what they're going to do to me.

"I might drop by to watch," she tells one guard, then she turns to me. "Oh, baby," she pouts. "You thought you could fool me because I'm a woman. You men just can't get it through your heads that we're smarter than you."

Damn. She's right, I shouldn't have . . . wait a fucking minute. I didn't underestimate her. I thought this was a shot in the dark at best. For a moment, my anger leaves and I feel a surge of pity.

"I didn't underestimate you. I'm not playing a game. I did the only thing I could think of to save my life. To save the life of my . . ."

I was going to say son, but I realize now I can't think that way. The biggest change I faced in becoming a parent was that my highest priority wasn't me anymore. In a real way, I was living for someone else, and their needs came first. It had been freeing, somehow easier. That kind of living seemed cleaner, less selfish and more fulfilling.

Beyond the heartbreak, the grieving, the unbearable loss of that thing which means the most to a person's heart, I guess it's the return to selfishness which is the true hallmark of a father who's lost his only son.

"I think I will find time to watch you break," Igraine says. "Maybe I'll even have them switch out kruks on you."

"I don't even know what a kruk is," I tell her, "so you can save your breath."

She turns away and walks back to the table. "Don't worry. It's worse than you're imagining, Cris. I'm sorry, but Maab has proven this is the best way. You're a danger to yourself, to others. Your ego makes you lie and take up airs. But this will humble you."

They drag me away.

Maybe, if I were healed, I could have fought these guards and beaten them before help had time to come. Maybe.

But now . . .

Now I'm just helpless.

XVI

Tintagel, it turns out, does indeed go deeper. Much deeper.

As we pass through guarded gates and descend down spiral stairways, I see a much different kind of slave here. These are definitely miners, and almost none of them could ever be confused with a sexual slave. They are horribly malnourished, closer to Auschwitz victims than to the men above, and are dressed in a lighter grey cloth which is both cut poorly and clumsily seamed. It is a caste system of slavery, I realize. Different flavors of horror, getting worse and worse as we go deeper, an awkward mimicry of the Hell outside this place.

After we come down one tight stairwell, the men become so emaciated I doubt they could have even survived on Earth. Their work is slower, and many we pass are simply panting by the rock, struggling to summon enough energy to lift their meager picks.

One man looks up at me, and I'm too stupid to look away. His eyes bug out from his wan, pale face. Dirt, not color, is what gives definition to the hollow of his cheeks. His fingernails are either bruised, battered and broken, or missing altogether. His open robe reveals a distended stomach, filled with gas in the perverse likeness of a full belly. His thin lips, pulled back by the tautness of his skin, reveal long teeth set weakly into receded gums.

They've castrated him.

"Wait," I tell the guards who drag me, but they do not listen.

How? How could people, people who assumedly had known the wonders of the 20th century, stand to see men in such a state?

"How can you do this to them?" I ask the guards.

"They do it to themselves," one answers.

And I remember, on Earth, how Myla had tried to explain why people who didn't love God, or believed in a different God than she, were choosing to go to Hell.

"If it's my choice," I had said, "then I choose not to go there."

"It doesn't work like that," she had answered.

And it doesn't.

Look at me.

Damned.

Myla, though, how had she ended up in Hell? Was it really her suicide that caused God to turn his back on her? But the longer I've been damned, the more skeptical of this I've become. It seems like all people go to Hell. Of course, I must be wrong. There must be a Heaven. Where else had that Angel come from? And maybe, just maybe, I should regret not loving Jesus. Or Vishnu. Or whichever God was the right one.

The universe couldn't be so cruel as to make sentient animals just to torture them.

But it can be that cruel.

And it just might be crueler than that.

We come to a pair of darkly dressed soldiers who strip search me again. It seems ridiculous, but then I remember that trick I'd performed to free myself from my bonds. They might think I have something on me.

My two guards stand watch as the new pair do their invasive search. When they're done, they don't put my clothes back on.

The room they lead me into is shaped like the inside of a well, and its cylindrical space seems to have been carved into whetstone.

A mirror—I'm presuming it's one way—rings around the top wall, flush with the ceiling. One small section of that mirror is a clear window, and I see up through it at an awkward angle. There is purple light beyond, but I can see little else.

At the bottom of the well, on the ground level where they take me, is a table.

There are shackles.

I'm only moments away from torture. I console myself with the fact that Durgan won't be doing this. These guys might be able to inflict more damage, and cause more pain, but at least I won't have to suffer humiliation in front of the wight's black eyes.

Though the Carrion cold has been largely missing in Igraine's compound, it completely saturates this room. I cannot say, however, if the goosebumps that rise on my arms come from cold or fear.

What can they do to me? I'd seen that they've castrated men. They might amputate my foot. That would be nice. Tooth pain, that's a bitch. They might drill into my mouth. They could put needles through my eye. Or remove fingernails.

And they could wait for me to regrow these things and do it again. But I probably won't face all that now. They need me to show them Blood Pass. Needles to one eye, the tooth drilling, fingernail removal, these things can all still happen, but they probably won't cut off my limbs or blind me.

Igraine had said they would leave me alive.

The guards chain me face down against the table. The ankle shackle closes with such force that the pain makes me lightheaded. My wrists are also shackled to the forward edges of the table. They're adjustable, which is nice, just in case I get taller or shorter from their ministrations. I'm able to look left and right, but at the moment there is nothing to see.

The cold of the stone and metal seeps into me while I wait. My balls hurt, but I can't do much to keep them warm. The temperature will probably be good for my ankle, though.

Then the guards leave, and the door slams, and I'm all alone.

Waiting.

Dreading.

Hair standing on end.

Don't think about what they're going to do to you. Just don't.

You'll deal with it when it comes.

I'm shaking.

It's from the cold.

I'm not afraid.

I can withstand torture.

A part of me wishes it would start, just so I know what they'll do. I've never really been tortured before. I mean, a little bit by Xyn and all.

But . . .

I attempt to silence the part of myself which wants to know my future. I try to calm down, to ease the pounding in my chest, to imagine something that will pacify my mind. I think of oceans and green fields, but old world things only remind me I'm in Hell—and all my memories of damnation are tainted. All of them.

The river and the brineberry bushes.

Myla.

Aiden.

All that has been made terrible, and I doubt I can have peace.

The door opens and a cruel light shines into my room. I hear voices from beyond, too quiet to make out, and then I catch the last few words.

"He's all yours, Melvin. Remember, he needs to live."

Melvin is one of the naked sex slaves, except he's not wearing any makeup on his face. He's sporting an erection.

They're going to rape me.

But that's not so bad. It's not like tooth drilling.

My legs are shaking so badly that the shackle is fucking up my ankle. I can't show fear. I'm supposed to be a God damned infidel.

But nobody believes that anymore.

They know me.

I'm nothing. A trickster. A liar whose lies have failed.

Melvin walks around, his midsection level with my eyes. I don't dare look at the thing he's going to penetrate me with.

It's okay. He's going to fuck me, and it's going to hurt like the worst shit ever, and I'll get over it. I'll heal. And then—

He bends down, his blue eyes looking into mine.

"Hey, baby," I say.

"I like your scent," he whispers.

Then he licks my forehead, where a cold sweat has broken out, and I feel the rough stubble of his beard on the bridge of my nose and the back of my eyelid.

His breath, lingering and rotten, makes me want to puke.

"You're tasty, too," he says in a nasal voice, and then he inhales deeply in through his nose.

Calloused hands, perhaps toughened from mining work, trace strange circles across my back as he walks around the table.

The shackles rattle from my fear.

I can't let this happen.

No. Cris, there's nothing he can do to you. You aren't less of a person because of something someone else does. Rape is a lie. It doesn't mean what people think it means, it's his problem, not—

He's climbed up on the table, and I feel the hairs of his chest on my back.

I jerk against the irons, chains jingle and my foot explodes with pain, but I can't get away. His stubble rubs my shoulder and then my neck, and then he's kissing my back, like a woman should, his chapped lips harsh against my suddenly vulnerable skin.

"I hear you like to roleplay," Melvin says, his pinched voice ending with a chuckle. "I tell you what, you be an infidel, and I, I'll be me."

One of his calloused hands reaches between my legs and fondles me roughly.

I grit my teeth and grunt as his grip tightens. Then his kisses return and I feel the stiffness of him pressing into my left buttock.

"Stop!" And I shake and shake and shake, but it does nothing.

I try to writhe away, but my range of motion is so limited I don't even know if he notices.

His breathing gets heavier and heavier, and the spittle from his wet kisses drips down my neck.

He starts nibbling on my ear while he prepares me with a finger.

"Stop," I whisper.

Rape is a lie. What he does to me doesn't lessen me as a person. It doesn't. It's his problem, not mine. His. He should be better.

I'm still worthwhile.

I'm just a trickster. Myla was right.

I got lucky, once, killing Xyn, and everything else has been a failure.

The finger digs deeper inside, giving me the odd feeling I have to shit.

Instinctively I clench, but that's the wrong thing to

do.

"Oh, sweetie," he says, removing his finger. "You're a virgin, aren't you?"

He puts the finger in front of my face.

"Smell it."

I hold my breath.

Then the finger goes and he presses himself into me, starting to penetrate me.

Don't give in, Cris. You have to do something.

But there is only one thing I can do, one act of defiance.

I shit all over his dick.

It's a diarrhea shit too, and loads of gas escape with the gushes of liquid feces.

"Oh motherfucker!" Melvin shouts, and he slams a fist into the back of my neck.

I have a moment of near unconsciousness, but then I hear the door open.

"I need a fucking bucket!" Melvin is yelling. "It fucking burns."

I start to laugh, and I feel some relief, but it ends up coming out as sobs as my stomach clenches.

Melvin is not gone long.

"Just lube for me, fucker," he tells me.

"Okay, shit dick," I say, but my voice waivers when I say it.

Then he violates me truly, and I cry, and it hurts, and he begins the slow process of taking away from me what it means to be a human being.

"You deserve this," Myla tells me as I'm rocked back and forth.

"No I don't," I insist.

"Yes you do."

The men I'd killed, and turned, just so she would die.

Yes I do.

I do deserve this.

I do.

I do.

I do.

XVII

I feel hollow inside, as if he'd carved out a place in my intestines, but I feel full there at the same time, as if I need to shit—but I don't. His semen and the blood from my own ripped asshole leaks out of me slowly, mixing with the dried shit caked to the insides of my thigh.

I can smell it all.

Melvin, perhaps sated, is breathing against my neck and ear. I struggle again, for all the good it does me.

His sweat drips onto my neck and back as he stands up, the slick sound of his skin rubbing on mine filling my ears. He moves in front of me and begins washing himself with the bucket and sponge.

He's getting aroused again.

I just want this to be over. I wish I could sleep until this was over.

Like Igraine did, he pets my cheek. Then he leans in and nibbles on my ear. "Don't worry. I've got another one in me. And then I'll call for back up. We'll be gentle with you, we don't want your insides ruptured too much."

My ass is split, like the motherfucker of all hemorrhoids.

But you can't defile a person. You just can't.

You're not supposed to be able to. Because I have to be the one that makes me less of a person. He's not allowed.

But inside me something has died.

And I know it.

And not even I have a delusion ready to deny it.

So Melvin takes me again, and then his two boys do, and then he leaves. And they wash me, and someone inspects my ass and says the damage is superficial, and that Melvin can come again tomorrow.

And they say that the next day.

And the next.

XVIII

"I was raped once." Her voice comes to me from above.

I struggle weakly against my irons. They clink a little. My neck is sore, so I try to turn my head to the other side. It's too stiff. I can't move it. I just lie there in pain. And compared to the agony of my insides, do I really care about my neck?

"Oh," she says, and the concern in her voice seems genuine, "are you crying?"

Of course I'm not crying.

No wait. I am. I must have been crying in my sleep.

Soft, slender fingers and the subtle touch of their fingernails find the knot in my neck. They dig into that piece of agony. This is pain too, but a good kind. As my neck considers loosening under her warm ministrations, I hear the cartilage of my back and shoulders popping and cracking. Relief floods that part of me, but the false need to defecate, and the utter pain of my ripped rectum and my bruised, swollen prostate are too primal for it to matter.

At least I don't know anyone anymore. At least no one will see me like this.

Her fingers continue their work, moving along my back. I didn't know I was this tense. Finally, I'm able to turn my head to the other side. She comes to one knee, her black robe rustling as she brings herself down to my level.

She has sharp, Asian features—Japanese heritage, perhaps. Her hair, black in a way that a Caucasian's cannot be, falls straight, almost disappearing against the sable of her cloak. Thin, blood-red lips purse as she studies me.

My face is swollen, I can feel the bruising on and around my cheekbones, and my left eye has only partial vision. I must look like a monster to her.

But I'm not. I'm a victim.

It's like the utter disgust I felt for Melvin has somehow been implanted into my insides with his sperm.

My body shakes as it tries to wretch, but it has nothing left to give.

"I know how you feel." Her lips move before my

eyes.

There is no trace of accent in her voice. My ankle hurts. My balls ache. My stomach muscles are cramping, and that causes movement in areas which very much need to be still right now.

"But if you think about it, you deserve this, you know?" she asks. "Now that you know how it feels to be treated this way, you can probably think about your own life. About what you did in the old world to make you responsible for something like this. Maybe it was the flippant way you treated a joke, or the way you tacitly agreed with the objectification of a girl."

I try to get my stomach to stay tense, but it won't. It fucking won't.

Her fingers move farther down my back, and the muscles she relaxes there send shockwaves of agony up through my body as my insides are allowed to shift.

"To men, it seems like such a foreign concept," she goes on, "this idea that minor words might cause something so terrible. Maybe watching cartoons will make one child in a million hit another with a mallet, who knows? But if one joke in a million causes rape, or if it even contributes to one, that's too many. You know that now. I mean, you guys usually understand why it's not okay to joke about genocide. But now that you've felt this—and believe me, this isn't the worst part—you know what you've done. Think back. Is there a time you pressured some girl to sleep with you? Maybe you lied about how committed you were, denying her right to properly consent?"

Her fingers get lower and lower, and the shifting of my insides becomes unbearable. I shout out. The effort that shout takes wounds me even more fundamentally. Even breathing ruins me. I try to breathe as shallowly as possible to keep everything in place.

"Now that this is real to you, you'll know it can happen again. The worst will come in a few months. It's when you realize what parts of you, of your soul, aren't healing. When you realize something, some piece of your autonomy or purity or self-respect or wholeness has been taken, and you won't ever get it back."

Her fingers find my left buttock, and I shout in pain again as she begins working on that muscle.

"Don't worry," she says. "Don't worry."

The relaxation continues and I hear gas bubbling out of my insides. Liquid cum and shit and clotted blood, trapped there by my swelling, now release themselves. I'm too tired to move or fight against the agony.

"Help me," I whisper.

She circles around the table and stops for a second time before my face. She lowers herself again so I can see her perfect features.

"I think another session with Melvin would endanger your life," she says. "And I know Igraine wants you to face another few sessions after we return, so you're going to have to heal on our journey. Do you understand?"

I can't take more of this. I have to find a way to die.

Her eyes, black in the dim light, seem like a wight's for a second, but then she looks up to the ceiling, and I see the white in them.

"This is your home now," she says thoughtfully. "You've seen how the slaves live. How things are down here, where you belong. And you've seen how much better they have it above. And you've seen the soldiers, the men who've gone through the baptism."

I have.

"Do you care what gods you pray to?" she asks.

I shake my head.

"Good," she says. "I like your body, and I'd enjoy taking what Myla had. You'll have to do some severe penance because you royally pissed Igraine off, but I can put in a bid to own you, if you want. You could be one of mine. It would take a lot of work to get you to be my consort, but wouldn't that be worth working for?"

I look at her. She really cares about me. She doesn't have to care. But she does. She thinks I'm attractive. I'm so grateful.

I nod my head quickly and tears spill out from my eyes.

"It won't be easy," she says. "You'll have to be a good boy and show me Blood Pass. Do you think you can do that for me? I might be allowed to keep you then."

I nod again.

"Good. You'll address me as Domina, you understand?"

"Yes," I manage.

She raises one eyebrow.

"Yes, Domina."

"Good boy. Now stay here. I'll see if I can't get you some rest someplace soft and warm before we go."

"Yes, Domina."

She really is beautiful.

After another session, they lay me down upon a couch with velvet cushions.

I'm shaking.

Domina kneels beside me, her face concerned. "I'm sorry, baby. There was nothing I could do to stop them from hurting you. And they're going to keep on hurting you. But if you're a good boy, and you do what I say, someday I can make sure they don't hurt you so much. Do you understand?"

"Yes, Domina."

I want nothing more than to curl up into a fetal position and cry, but bending my midsection causes feelings in my insides I don't want to have. Slowly, inch by inch, I dare it.

And after an hour of effort, after my back eases and the warmth of the cushions sinks into my body, I'm able to finally curl into a ball.

There's food when I awaken. I'm starving, I need it—but I don't dare. I'm provided with a grey shirt of the same color as the slave robes. After some concerted effort, I'm able to get it on.

A Little Lady comes, a blonde girl, maybe seven years old. "You better eat it," she says. "Shy will be mad if you don't."

I don't know who Shy is.

"You want to disappoint your Domina?" the Little Lady asks.

"No."

I can't afford to disappoint her. She's the only one who wants to stop the pain.

My stomach growls angrily as I eat and drink.

I don't dare shit. I try to hold it.

The Little Lady comes back and makes me eat again, and I hold it.

And I hold it.

"You're not so pretty anymore," she says.

My stomach is swollen.

She's right. Domina only likes me because my body, unlike most of the slaves', looks good. Or looked good. Eating food I can't shit out isn't going to make me any more attractive.

And Igraine wants me punished. By the time her anger ebbs, and Domina can finally make a play for me, she might not even want to.

Fuck.

This is so fucked.

I hold it.

I hold it.

She comes again, and I eat.

And I hold it.

Shitting hurts so bad I pass out from the pain. I hadn't even meant to do it. It just happened. I almost made it to the chamber pot. The Little Lady makes a slave clean up my feces. She makes him do it with his tongue.

He looks at me, his dark eyes full of the hate and ire he dare not express to a priestess, as the brown of my shit stains the sleeves and knees of his grey robe.

"You didn't get any on the Domina's couch," the Little Lady congratulates me. "You really are trying to be a good boy, aren't you?"

I nod.

Of course I am. Anything less and I'd be licking my own shit up off the floor.

I eat.

For the sake of my poor compatriot, I shit in the pot.

You're welcome, buddy.

Again come her relaxing fingers.

"We should wait until he's good enough to walk," a male voice says as Domina works on me.

His accent is odd. African, maybe? South African?

"That's what Fellman is for," says Domina.

"Blood Pass isn't going anywhere."

"Nor is he. Igraine says he has a knack for escaping bonds."

"We'll have the hound. We can track him and kill him if he escapes."

"I told you," Domina whispers, "I don't want him dead."

"It's because you've fallen for Myla."

"You can be unbaptized, you know." Her voice silences him.

The Little Lady wakes me. "I have a map."

I'm still curled up. I move over and look down at the floor where she's spread it out. I see nothing I recognize—wait, there's Maylay Beighlay, its name scrawled over a city by the top right edge.

And there's the Erebus. Seeing the line which represents the river of darkness reminds me of something Neb said long ago, in his castle of ice, which I'd nearly forgotten. My son will still be near the Erebus. He has to move away from it slowly so he has time to heal.

Aiden is by the river. Or at least had been, God knows how long I've been here.

Cid and Q, even if they'd managed to follow me all the way to the stadium chamber, would be long gone. Aiden might still be on the banks, though . . . but if he sees me like this . . .

My heart sinks.

"What's the last thing you remember about leaving Blood Pass?" she asks.

I think.

I remember us passing through a rubble wall. That was a Carrion barrier, I bet. It's just my stupid ass didn't know what the Carrion was back then. Okay, I also remember some smooth caverns. Very smooth. Ares had said something about Vyn worms making them.

I remember that because it reminded me of my friend, Vinny, in the old world.

I scour the map. I see them, there, Vyn caverns. They are surprisingly close to the Erebus. That makes sense. The City of Blood and Stone is deep into the Carrion, and Ares had basically taken a bee line out of the place.

But there's got to be an easier way to find Blood Pass. What can I remember before we made it to the barrier? Surely there are some features that might give us a better starting point at least.

No.

You're stupid. You're not here to take them to Blood Pass. You're here to escape.

But escaping like this would mean nothing. I'd die

in minutes.

And I can't take care of my son like this . . . unless. They did let Durgan into Tintagel, so this might be the best place for Aiden, short of another Archdevil.

That's it then—we're going back to the banks of the Erebus. The shame I'll feel at seeing him, I'll have to swallow it. Maybe Shy can own both me and Aiden, and then all three of us can be evil together.

I point. "There, by the Erebus, that's where Myla and I came out. That circular hallway, I believe there are crystals that light up when we walk. We need to start there."

We can find my son, and then I can make up some lie to get us to the Vyn caverns.

She looks at me with her blue eyes. "That's a long way, mister."

For a second, she reminds me of Jenner. "I'm sorry. I've been thinking, and I thought the map might help. But I need to get back there. It's the part I remember the best."

But this decision, this path, it might be the right one, but it could still have consequences. "Will Domina be mad?"

This seems to put the Little Lady at ease. "I don't think so. Just don't mess up."

I'm coming for you, Aiden. I may be the biggest fuck up of a father in all damnation, but I'm coming.

I smell oil and steel.

A man has entered my room. His skin is a deep black, so dark it nearly looks blue, and he's wearing chainmail. A god damned rapier hangs by his side. Long dreadlocks, bound together behind his head, flow over his mailed shoulders. At his side is a hellhound. It's a small one, only two feet tall or so. It has a leather harness and a muzzle. The poor thing's throat has been shaved, so I assume they recently cut out its vocal cords. It walks awkwardly, and I realize that each of its front knuckles have been removed.

What the fuck is the point of having a hellhound that can't bark or claw?

It manages a whine, so maybe I'm wrong about its vocal cords.

Its eyes roll oddly. Are they drugging the thing too? Weird.

"You know the way to Blood Pass?" the man asks, his voice colored with the South African accent I'd heard earlier.

I nod.

"Good."

The Little Lady enters next, and like the South African, she's also got a leash with her, or rather, four leashes. But instead of hellhounds on the ends of them, she has grey-robed slaves.

She has the slaves kneel beside me, setting the ends of their leashes down, one by one, on the stone floor before moving to speak to the black man.

I recognize the hateful dark eyes of one of slaves. Brown still stains his robe, but only faintly. I'm sorry, brother. I am. I didn't know.

"You're going to try resisting Shy," one slave tells me prophetically in a low tone, his head still bowed.

I don't know what to say, or how to answer. Would I try? Maybe if I can't trick them into finding Aiden. In this state, I can't defend myself, but I might enjoy dying.

"You are," he says. "You're new. Everyone wants to escape at first. The penalty is the table, but you're going to get that anyway. Look, serf, I've got a line on a Domina. I was a thrall, but my kruk died. You try to take her down the wrong path, and we run into devils, guess who's going to die?"

"I don't know," I whisper.

There is a long pause.

"We are," Shit-eater says. "They set us loose at the first sight of devils, and use our deaths as cover."

He turns to regard the Little Lady, clearly afraid that she might have heard him.

"I know you want to fight," the first slave continues, "but realize that we're the ones who will die for your petulant little rebellion."

I try to let this soak in, but it's hard to care who lives and who dies.

"Who's the black fellow?" I ask.

"Din," Shit-eater says. "He's one of Lucreas'

disciples. He and Gilgamesh are learning how to control the hounds."

"We owe him a lot," the other slave says. "Those hounds can sense devils. Less of us have been killed lately."

Three soldiers enter next, Carrion born, their shotguns slung over their shoulders like rifles. Belts, full of shells, line their midsections. They look so cruel. If I'm lucky enough, and Domina can make me one of them, will I look as evil?

The idea of becoming so hateful hurts me, but I think I'm willing to do it, or to pretend to do it. Anything to save me from Melvin.

The thought of that man, of his bad breath and stubble sends a shiver down my spine, and that shiver hurts my insides.

At last my Domina enters with a tall, lanky man at her side, dressed as a slave but with well-defined muscles.

Well, lanky may not quite cover it. His torso belongs on a much shorter man, and his spindly limbs seem almost comical in comparison. His movement is devoid of grace, and he's a little hunched—but still, the man is clearly strong.

"That's my charge?" the gangly giant asks, pointing a tree-like limb and twig-like finger my way.

Domina nods.

He walks to me, arms swinging, and pulls out a

harness. "My name's Fellman," he says. "I'll be your legs."

So this is the group then. My Domina, her Little Lady, three soldiers, Din the houndsman, Fellman to carry me, and of course, the four slaves who will be bait.

Poor bastards.

But then again, I'm pretty sure I have it worse.

Fellman puts me on his back and straps me in, surprisingly careful not to hurt my ankle.

Din grins, white teeth flashing, and gives me a wink.

I don't have the heart to make a faithful steed joke. Fellman jumps a little, and hikes me higher on his back. The motion puts pressure on my split anus and bruised insides. My right ankle is shaken.

It's a good thing I'm being carried, because I'm pretty sure I just gave up.

We do not leave through the waterfall, but instead
climb out from under a flagstone which reminds me, in
an odd way, of climbing up through an old world sewer
grate.

Fellman has no trouble negotiating the upward
climb, and my back brushes against the stone opening
only briefly.

I try to give them directions, but my Domina
shushes me with a single raised finger. They are not
following my lead yet. They won't until we leave the
Carrion, I bet. But despite this, in short order, we are
walking back along halls I'm sure I recognize. This is
the way that Durgan took us. Maybe he learned the

path from the Carrion born, or maybe this is the only safe way to go.

Domina walks, the Little Lady at her heel, surrounded on all four corners by her leashed slaves. Fellman carries me just ahead of them. Two Carrion born take up the lead at the front, while the third lags behind as a rearguard. They rotate from time to time because apparently being in the back sucks.

I just have to trust the guard behind us because it hurts for me to look backward.

As we travel, the straps of the harness start digging into my thighs and shoulders, and the abominable soreness of my neck returns. I rest my head on Fellman's shoulder.

His face, perhaps an inch away, cocks to the side so one of his eyes is looking at me. "Don't worry, sweetheart, we'll get to a safe house tonight."

That at least, is something.

Between myself and the front two soldiers is Din and his hound. The dog's nose gives us a huge advantage over the devils. At times, Din raises his hand, and we seek cover amidst the shadows.

I begin to become ambivalent about the devils. Let them find us. We deserve to die.

Now that I'm no longer terrified, I have time to worry about the future.

I don't think I can handle the walk back through Blood Pass, if I can even find it. I don't think I can face those places where Myla and I sat together, holding each other, loving each other, when damnation was a new and untested thing. How could something so beautiful have gone so wrong?

Look at me. This is what happens to a man who loses his true love. Who loses the purpose of his life.

Who loses.

We come to what looks like a dead end, but Din steps forward, his chainmail nearly silent, and puts his hands into the space between two hellstone bricks. Then, with tremendous effort, he pulls to the right. The wall itself, I realize now, is actually a giant stone wheel, and it grinds with a low rumble as it rolls slowly aside.

We enter, Fellman carrying me as the Carrion born wheel the wall shut behind us all.

Beyond the door, corridors spiral inward, around and around, and I get dizzy with the turns Fellman makes as we travel toward the center of the complex for what seems like a mile. At the end, a carpeted room awaits. Fellman unbuckles my harness and places me on the floor.

"You've got a good buffer," the Little Lady says. "You don't have to worry about staying quiet."

Then she, Domina and Din leave, going back the way we entered, perhaps to make sure the complex was clear or to discuss some business.

The walls are stained with grime and smoke,

though I'm not sure who would start a fire over carpet. The carpet itself is the kind you'd find in an old world public building. Tiny colorless fibers are knitted together, forming little pods that spread out before me like a miniature, grey-treed forest. Such an odd thing to find in Hell.

The carpet has absorbed the Carrion cold. I can't stand up, both because of my insides and because of my ankle, so I crawl toward a corner.

Fellman laughs.

"What a cute widdle puppeh!" the gangly man says in an affected, high-pitched voice.

I don't make it to the corner. Shit-eater blocks my path. His metal collar is bolted around his neck, but he's taken off his leash. He clips it to my shirt.

"Bark, little dog," he orders.

I roll to one side. This isn't the kind of thing I can deal with right now.

The three guards and the slaves are laughing.

"I think you have to feed him a treat," one soldier says. "This dog isn't too well trained."

Shit-eater turns to Fellman. "You want to give the dog a little snack?"

Fellman's gangly hands drop to his belt. He undoes his pants.

Fucking Jesus, not again. Not again.

He's already erect, and he waves his thin, crooked dick at me.

Shit-eater bends down so his face is only a foot away from where I lay. "You going to bark, doggy? Are you?"

He stands tall, steps back, and kicks me in the midsection.

Pain.

I think I just fainted for a minute.

Sweat stands out on my forehead and my insides feel wrong, as if they've turned to liquid. That terrible pressure on my innards has returned.

He's got my pants down around my knees, and my ankle is also on fire.

"Bark!" he shouts, pulling me up to a kneeling position.

Fellman steps toward me, filling my vision.

"You can't," I manage to say before my next breath. "Domina will be mad. You can't. I might die."

The room erupts with laughter. Their cruel faces look down at me. One of the other slaves kicks me. With my pants down, restricting my balance, the kick topples me over. Instinctively, I try to get my asshole pointed away from Fellman.

It appears that in whatever caste system they have, I'm less than even a slave.

"Bark!" Shit-eater yells. "Get on your knees and bark."

I look to the exit. Domina has to be coming soon. She has to save me.

"Bark!"

Another kick clips my head.

I start to cry.

Shit-eater mimics my tears, sniffling. "Little doggy's all sad."

The soldiers join him, mocking me, letting out great howling guffaws at my misery.

I just want to die.

I can't take it again.

Slowly, I crawl to my knees, my arms shaking, tears falling off my face to darken small parts of the carpet.

I bark.

"Say woof, motherfucker!" Shit-eater yells, ecstatic.

He readies another kick.

"Woof," I say.

"Louder!"

"Woof!" I try, but shouting hurts my stomach.

They laugh and laugh and laugh.

"Roll over!" one soldier demands.

I try to pull my pants up, but Fellman reaches down and stops me. "Oh no, don't be a bad dog. Do you want to be a bad dog?"

I remain silent.

"Do you?" his face, despite the length of his limbs, seems to have been all scrunched together.

"No."

He smiles at me, a grin full of even teeth under his

button nose. "You want to be a good dog, don't you, boy?"

"I do."

"Roll over!"

So I roll over.

And the laughter hurts my ears.

One of the other slaves comes forward, standing over me, looking down on me. He's the one who asked if I'd resist my Domina.

"Sit!" he orders.

So I sit.

"Beg!" another calls.

So I beg.

"Bark!"

So I bark.

And they laugh.

And laugh.

And laugh.

I see her enter the room, my Domina. My heart swells. She needs me alive, she's said as much, she can't let this continue.

She shakes her head and rolls her eyes.

And of course she would. She only wants me as her slave because she's attracted to me. Because I can bring her pleasure. But how could she be attracted to a man like me? Helpless and defiled. Out of control. Malnourished. Broken.

What woman has ever been attracted to such

things?

How could I ever recover from a moment like this in her eyes?

Fellman tires of the game. He picks me up.

"No!" Shit-eater says. "You're ruining it."

"For you," Fellman says. "My fun just started."

He carries me like some kind of bride into one of the dark, stone-floored rooms connected to this chamber. He lays me down, and enters me. I feel the pressure of him much more on my left side than my right. He works, and sweats, and grunts while I cry. Then he finishes, and holds me in his arms.

I can't do anything.

I'd want to reach between my own legs and destroy his balls, but they'd grow back, and he has to carry me tomorrow.

So I sit there, feeling the heat of his body, and his warm breath on my neck.

The cold seeps into me from the stones and the shivering hurts me.

The only thing I can do to stop that pain is to move back into Fellman and accept his body heat.

But I'm too proud for that, aren't I?

No.

No I'm not.

The night, his even breath, the momentary condensation which cools my neck in between those warm blasts, the heat of his body, the press of his limp genitals against my buttock, the foreign arm around my midsection, it lasts forever.

We travel through the day, and at night, we find no set of safe chambers. Instead we find a small cavern, much like the ones Durgan had us sleep in, and I bed down against the cold stone. Fellman lowers my pants and moves to take me, here, in the room with everyone. My asshole splits again as he enters, and the blood makes the raw feeling a little less painful.

"Please," I beg.

"Please what?" he asks, his voice amused.

I don't know what to say.

"You want me to be gentle, don't you?" he asks.

My soul twists, and tears start leaking out of my eyes. I nod.

"Say it, or I won't be."

"Be gentle."

And he is.

As we wake and they prepare to leave, I'm left alone on the cold stone floor. As always, the shivering hurts my insides. I begin to wonder if the short rape is worth the heat. Maybe I should thank Fellman a little.

One of the slaves gives me what I think is an empathetic glance. He'd tortured me before, when they'd made me pretend to be a dog, with the others. Still, I don't think he quite meant it. I think he just dared not show any softness amidst such company.

I miss the days when it was just Durgan banging my ankle into the walls.

They heft me up, harness me in, and we travel again.

Din drugs his hound with some laced food, and then, right after the dose, a dyitzu appears. Din rapiers it through the eye before Domina can even release her slaves.

It falls dead to the floor, its devil blood spilling out.

Wordlessly, I'm carried on.

The slaves are white as ghosts.

I fall into a near doze, and wait, hoping for death to come. I'm awakened by the whispering accented voice of Din.

"My hound doesn't want to go this way."

"It smells the harpy nest," Domina whispers back. "There's no need to fear, though. The harpies are gone. You can tell because there's no sting in the air."

Only because Ryan mentioned it before, I can smell the pomegranate.

If I stay silent, we might go into the nest, and I might die. Probably not. They'd scatter the slaves and make a run for it. But they might die.

But Domina doesn't deserve that. Shit-eater certainly does, and Fellman, but the others . . . I just don't know.

I look to the slave man, the one who asked me to spare his life.

"Pomegranate," I whisper.

"Quiet," Fellman hushes me.

"Domina," I say just loud enough for her to hear.

Fellman turns his head, his nose touching my cheek, as he issues a harsh whisper, "I said quiet."

"What is it?" Domina asks.

"These harpies, they use pomegranate to mask themselves. We discovered it with Keith and his men. The hound is right."

Domina and Din share a look.

She sniffs the air.

"I can't smell shit," Fellman says.

Domina cocks her head to one side. "But I can. We go around."

She reaches out with one hand and touches my

cheek. "You were a very good boy, just now. A very good boy."

My body shakes with the pleasure of hearing her words.

I'm going to have to hang on. If I can get her a wight *and* show Domina Blood Pass, it might redeem me in her eyes. She might see me as capable. As worth having. As something other than a receptacle for Fellman's lust and jism.

We lay down in the bones that night, in one of the enclaves of the catacombs, and Fellman takes me. He's not gentle, his thrusts knocking my face against the wall repeatedly and cracking some of the dried ribs we lie in.

I look at the dead and pretend I'm a skeleton too, shifting with them, just empty bones, no flesh, no soul, no feelings.

I catch Domina's eye. Her look of disgust cuts me to the quick.

I'll be useless in her world. These slaves, they have to fight for their food. They have to assert their dominance to win every bite. I doubt I'll be any good at that.

Fellman shifts, and my head is no longer being rammed into the wall. That's something.

I catch a glimpse of a skull, dark eyeless sockets staring at me. There is a very distant possibility that this head belongs to the ribcage I found myself holding the last time I slept in one of these rooms. I'm rocked back and forth toward the sockets. I close my eyes and pretend I'm somewhere else.

Fellman finishes.

His breathing becomes a constant on my neck. The gentle rhythm of the rise and fall of his chest lulls me into the embrace of sweet, sweet nightmares. On Earth, they'd said a man who died in his dreams would die in reality. Wouldn't that be nice.

I try not to jerk in my sleep because that would disturb Fellman and make him angry.

He begins to snore.

They must think these catacombs are pretty safe because no one wakes him. I know I dare not.

I feel strangely secure—as if Fellman will protect me.

And that disgusts me.

But what choice do I have?

It's impossible to sleep like this, in the arms of an enemy, surrounded by evil soldiers and owned by a woman who barely protects me. Owned by a woman who shouldn't even *want* to protect me.

And the hours pass and pass.

And pass.

And pass.

The hound's head perks up, sniffing the air. Its eyes look more cogent than usual, and I realize it's been several hours since its last dose. I feel a low rumble which, for a second, I think is Fellman snoring, but it's the dog's growl. Then it emits a short whine.

Din sits straight up, awakened from his slumber. He looks around and quietly shakes the trio of Carrion born awake. Both the little lady and Domina already have their eyes open.

Din stands, his chainmail chinking softly, his pistol drawn at the darkness beyond our chamber. Fellman stirs, and the breathing on my neck stops. He clutches me tighter to him.

Domina, silent amidst her flowing black robes, rises, a Beretta pistol in her hand. Her preternaturally beautiful face is half covered in shadow, and I feel my soul stir. That woman is my protector. I must have faith in her.

Domina points at one soldier and then to the hallway. He crawls over the bones, which crunch and crackle, and then he steps up onto the three foot wall that divides our enclave from the hallway. He looks left, then right, then turns back to us and shrugs.

"It's not there now," Din says, studying his hound, "I doubt it passed us in the night, or the dog would have awakened. I bet it got close though, perhaps a chamber or two over."

Domina's eyes are fixed on the hallway. "Can you tell from the hound if it was human or devil?"

Din frowns. "No, but I think the hound's smelling something new. I've never seen him like this."

The Little Lady squeaks, "Should we scatter the slaves?"

Domina's eyes narrow. She is breathtaking. She must be a match for whatever devil is out there, particularly with the Carrion born and Din at her side.

"No," she says. "Quickly, move."

Fellman comes to his feet, scattering bones with a clatter. He gets the harness ready, and for the first time, I help him put it on me. He nods approvingly, and I feel some kind of bond with him. In this one thing, we are allied. The devils, they would do worse to me than he.

Wouldn't they?

Maybe not.

The slaves form up around Domina, handing her their leashes. The soldiers move gingerly out into the hallway, two going right and the third going left to guard our backs. Slowly Fellman, with me on his back, crawls out.

He comes to his feet, and I try to stay tight to him so he can keep his balance. Din and the slaves come out next, followed by Domina and the Little Lady. I turn back and forth, looking ahead and behind us into the darkness.

I see nothing.

Maybe the dog is crazy.

I hear the whistles of infidel fire behind us.

"Down!" I shout.

But Fellman turns around instead, looking back toward the whistling. A series of explosions goes off, their blasts echoing incessantly in the bone filled chambers. The effect is disorienting, and a sudden gust of air and gravel drives Fellman to his knees.

Infidels. There are infidels here?

Din and the rearguard Carrion born loose a few bullets toward the billowing dust which is heading right toward us.

But how are they here? Could this be Q and Cid? Domina took us down roughly the same route Durgan had taken. If Q had managed to follow Durgan to the stadium chamber, he would have lost our trail there. Is it possible they'd been waiting all this time?

"Hold your fire!" The Little Lady's high pitched voice is strangely audible against the reports of the gunfire and the settling of dust and stone.

Domina had not fallen to her knees. She hands her leashes to the Little Lady and walks back into the smoke, heedless of any danger.

"Turn around and face forward," the Little Lady orders. "They won't come through from behind with all that dust in the air."

Fellman obeys her, turning around, but I don't. I crane my neck so I can see Domina disappear into the cloud.

Slowly the dust around us thickens, and our visibility becomes very limited, not that we could see shit in the darkness anyway.

Domina's silhouette appears, picking its way back to us through the corridor, the dim light of an enclave projecting her shadow toward us through the clouded air. She clears the haze, a haughty expression etched onto her exquisite features.

"A collapse bars our retreat," she says. "I'm guessing our enemies meant to do that."

Fellman turns, making it easier for me to stare at her.

"We've only one way to go," she says. "Serfs first."

The four men line up, shoulder to shoulder in the cramped hall. They are fodder in the truest military sense, existing only so their deaths can grant the Carrion soldiers a few extra seconds to live. Together, almost in lockstep, they march forward.

We follow, Fellman's boots crunching in the gravel.

"I need to drug the hound," Din says.

"It can wait," the Little Lady whispers harshly.

"Not long," Din insists.

"Put it down if you have to," Domina says. "We're nearly out of the Carrion."

Din gives out a low, rumbling growl surprisingly

similar to his hound. "But we'll be going right back in."

"I told you, baptisms can be undone."

This silences him.

As we move, we clear the haze, and I see the archway where our hallway opens up to the stadium chamber. With all those thousands of entrances and hundreds of levels, that's got to be a great place for an ambush.

Domina's voice halts us at the entrance. "Stop."

And we do.

I can't see past their bodies, so I do my best to imagine the room beyond. Only, I don't know what floor we're on. Could this be the same path Keith took us down? The odds of that would be very, very low.

Domina speaks loudly, her voice echoing back along the hallway's enclaves and, I assume, out into the stadium chamber. "We're not coming out."

"It's okay," Cid's voice calls to us from beyond. "We have no intention of killing you. Leave our man by those two purple stones, and you can all walk away from this with your lives."

At hearing Cid's voice, I start to shake. I don't know why, but the sound hurts me for some reason. I think I want to cry.

"Not a chance, sweetheart," Domina calls back.

"We're infidels, we'll honor our word."

I hear the howling winds pick up in the stadium chamber.

"We've got food and time," Domina answers, "so you better be well-fed infidels."

Din chuckles at this.

Our soldiers are twitchy, though. I don't think they expected to be fighting a crew of infidels—but there isn't a crew, not really. Just Q and Cid.

One turns to Domina, his shoulders hunched with worry, and his mouth opens—

The Little Lady points her pistol at his face. "Do as you're told."

He shuts his mouth, and shaking with fear, turns back around.

"Neb," I hear Cid's voice say, "flush 'em out."

"*Guten Abend.*" Neb's voice is harsh and low.

A second series of explosions goes off, but this time with less effect. A loose cloud of dust settles all around us. It smells like something darkly familiar. Corpsedust? No. Wightdust? Definitely not.

It smells like moldy books—like the bottom floor of an old and leaky library.

We wait for more explosions, but none come.

Din starts chuckling, a high-pitched, foreign laugh. "I do hope you brought good provisions," he shouts, "or at least some working explosives."

Had their infidel fire failed them? An entire set at the same time? It could happen. If you get corpsedust on your weapons, it can certainly cause misfires—and that would explain the odd smell. Jesus Christ, my luck's turned bad.

Maybe the infidels aren't as good as I thought. Igraine hadn't seemed afraid of them. Maybe, just maybe, she was right about what it took to survive in the Carrion.

I let myself consider, for the first time, that the crew I'm with might be superior to Cid and Q. Certainly Q is quieter and a better tracker, but that hound has abilities to match his. And even if Cid is a better shot, would it matter since the slaves will allow Domina and Din extra time to aim their weapons?

But then Neb starts singing, and I feel the hairs on the back of my neck rise as his voice, pure and deep and blessed with a surprising vibrato, sounds out like hellsong down our halls.

"Guten Abend, gute Nacht,"

The German words are foreign to me, but the melody is that most classic of all lullabies.

"mit Rosen bedacht,

"mit Näglein besteckt,"

There is some clicking around us, from the bones. Fleshless skeletons cannot become corpses, so perhaps the explosion has disturbed something in these chambers. Spiders maybe, or some sort of rodent horde.

"Vermin!" Din shouts.

The soldiers unload a few rounds of buckshot into the catacomb chambers to our left and right. White puffs of bone dust plume up from each blast as shattered pieces of skeleton ricochet about the hallway. A dry, musty smell joins the mildewy odor of the last explosion.

All is still.

"Schlupf' unter die Deck!" Neb's singing continues as the dust keeps settling.

There is more twitching in the beds of bones, and whatever is crawling beneath the dead is disturbing a skeletal arm so that it looks like it's reaching for us.

More shotgun blasts ring out.

"Morgen früh, wenn Gott will,"

The arm keeps moving back and forth along the bones . . . oh God. Oh God. The bone hand lifts itself on the end of its skeletal arm, rising up out of the morass.

Oh good God almighty.

The arm bends, and the hand touches down onto the mass of bones. It shakes and rattles as its torso rises from the sea of the dead. A skull, attached to the end of that skeletal torso, turns to look at us.

"Wirst du wieder geweckt."

"They're rising," Din shouts, pointing into the right catacomb chamber.

"Skeletons don't rise." Domina's voice corrects him.

And I thought she was right. I really did. But apparently Neb knows better than she or I.

The dead are slow and clumsy, falling over themselves as jumbles of bones which combine and recombine, sometimes taking on different parts from other bodies.

"Domina!" the Little Lady screeches.

"We've got to move!" I tell Fellman.

Fellman begins to shake, almost violently. A skeletal hand reaches out over the squat wall divide and grabs at his thigh. He kicks at it, but as a slave, he has no weapons.

"Guten Abend, gute Nacht,"

"Fend them off!" Domina's voice is shrill, lacking any of its normal composure.

The soldiers try more buckshot, but that doesn't do shit. Din's rapier is all but useless, so he resorts to smashing at them with the hilt.

"They don't stay down!" a soldier shouts.

Fellman jerks away, ripping his pant leg out of the grip of a skeletal hand.

"von Englein bewacht,

"die zeigen im Traum . . ."

Farther back along the hallway, fully formed skeletons tumble over the waist-high walls and land in the chambers. On shaky legs they stand like newborn deer, and then, each jerky step uneven, they begin to shamble toward us. Their progress is terribly slow, but they're filling the hallway, so there won't be a lot Domina will be able to do about them when they get here.

"If you kill Cris, you all die," Q says. "But I'll only

shoot your legs. The dead will be the ones that take you."

"Damn it," Domina says, and then she shouts louder. "We're coming out! Don't shoot!"

The Little Lady's head whips around. "You can't!"

"Hush," Domina says, turning to Fellman. "There are tons of passages like this in the next chamber. When you get out, head toward the purple stones as if we're doing as they say, but—" her voice is drowned out by the panicked shouts of her Carrion born and a pair of shotgun blasts. "—and then hug the left wall. Do you understand me? Hug the left wall. Then I want you to sprint back down the next passage over. Do you understand?"

Fellman is nodding.

"Move!" Domina shouts.

We rush out into the stadium chamber, our soldiers releasing volleys of useless buckshot back at the undead. The whipping wind catches us, drowning out the clicking sound of bone on rock.

"There!" Domina points to a cluster of cubic purple stones. "Put his body there!"

Fellman rushes left, but stays close to the wall. I can't see any of my friends, but I realize that if they rescue me, they'll find everything out. They'll know what's happened.

Shame, deep and abiding, wells up from within me and suddenly I'm terrified of facing my friends. I'm afraid in a way I've never been before.

"Run!" Domina releases her leashes. "Now, Fellman!"

Fellman turns on his heel.

The slaves break in all directions, but there isn't a whole lot of room on this tier. One drops over the ledge, two are heading for the stairs on the left, the other for the stairs on the right. Cid and Q don't shoot them, though I wish they would.

The Carrion born loose some buckshot, firing helter-skelter around the tremendous chamber.

One drops, his head jerking backward in the opposite direction of his body. Fellman races back into a hallway with Din hot on our heels. Domina comes in next, a single Carrion born behind her.

"Fire a few more rounds," she orders the soldier, her composure regained. "Quickly, Din. We need to get down this passage and lose them in the lower levels."

She leads us at a jogging pace down this new corridor. Again, enclaves full of the dead flank us on the left and right. This time, thank God, they're not moving.

Domina's mask cracks again when her final Carrion born is shot down.

"Clear!" I hear Q's surprisingly close voice shout.

Behind us the infidel fire whistles.

"Down!" I yell at Fellman.

Again, he's too stupid to listen, and instead turns around. The blast isn't so bad, but the shaking after the explosion is enough to send Fellman and I to the floor.

Dust covers us over and fills the air.

I watch it swirl as I consider whether to attempt choking Fellman unconscious. If I succeed, then Domina will kill me. If I fail, then Fellman will hate me.

Maybe I shouldn't do anything.

Din's dark figure cuts through the dusty air, and the man helps Fellman—and me by proxy—to his feet.

"We need to run!" the Little Lady screeches. "They'll cut us off."

Domina turns as if she's about to follow the Little Lady's advice, but Din reaches out with one hand and grabs her wrist.

"We can't outrun them while carrying Cris," he says.

He and Domina's eyes meet.

A few of his dreadlocks have come loose, and he brushes them away from his face. "We need to surrender."

"No!" the Little Lady yells. "Igraine wants the pass. There can be no surrender. We can fight them off. Igraine will kill us if we lose him."

Domina doesn't look at her.

"Guten Abend, gute Nacht," Neb's baritone returns, not from the stadium chamber behind us, but from the catacombs ahead.

God, they've cut us off already.

"We're outmatched, Shy," Din says.

With a single smooth gesture Domina raises her Beretta and shoots the Little Lady in the head. Fellman jerks, and I can feel the tenseness of the rigid muscles in his back.

Domina moves toward me, putting her hand on my cheek and stepping around Fellman.

"You love me, don't you?" she asks.

I nod as Fellman's body goes slack. I'm in Domina's surprisingly strong arms. She grunts as Din works at the harness. Then I'm free, and Domina lowers me, ungracefully but slowly enough to where I'm not hurt, to the ground.

I'm entranced by her dark amber eyes.

She kneels beside where I lay and kisses me, like a lover might. "Someday you'll be mine," she promises, her whisper sending a thrill down my spine. "I want you to shout and tell your friends that you're okay. Can you do that for me?"

"It hurts when I shout." I say.

A soft concern for my wellbeing narrows her eyes. "You don't have to shout very loud, Cris. You want to be a good boy, don't you? This is very important."

"I do," I say. "I'll shout as loud as I can."

"Promise?"

"I promise."

She stands, and I see where Fellman has fallen, blood still pooling out from where Din's rapier had pierced him below the chin.

"Can you hear me?" Domina yells.

"Yes," Cid answers.

"There's two of us, your man is safe. Tell them you're safe, Cris."

"I am," I say, and then repeat louder. "I am."

"Come forward a few steps," Cid says. "An infidel will check to make sure he's okay. After he's cleared we'll let you go."

Domina smiles sadly. "We'll keep our weapons lowered, but I won't disarm. Your man will have to be okay with that as we pass him."

"No need," Q's voice says from behind us. "And no need for you to turn around either. If you do, you will die. Walk two steps forward, please."

Q's form is half obscured by the haze, but I see him now, his M-16 shouldered.

He knows. He saw me talking to Domina. He saw her kissing me. He knows what I've become.

I feel disgust in my stomach.

"Cris." Q's voice is tender with pity, so maybe he hasn't guessed everything yet. "Come to me."

He'll know soon enough. That infidel brain will be ticking. He'll see it. It's so obvious I've been polluted.

"Cris?" he asks.

Not like this. He can't see me like this. Domina, save me. Take me away.

"He can't walk." Domina's voice echoes about in my head.

Lukewarm blood from Fellman seeps into the hem of my long sleeve shirt.

Q's shadow takes another step through the haze. "Keep looking forward," he orders them, his words short and clipped.

Domina's black hair stirs as her head turns ever so slightly. That hair covers her eyes, but I can just barely see the ruby red of her lips as she whispers, "You can crawl to your friend."

I hurt so much inside.

Q's M-16 comes down an inch. "What did you do to him?"

Domina's shoulders tense, and it hurts me to see her afraid. I feel her pain in my gut.

Din is as still as rock.

Behind us, clicking along the stone, I hear the steps of the skeletons. Q came from back there, so the stadium chamber entrance hasn't been blocked off by this explosion.

The dead are out there, and they can get to us.

Q comes out of the mist to stand over me, his nostrils flared, eyes wide with anger, his body armor rising with his heavy breathing. This time his voice sounds well controlled. "What did you do?"

Domina's head turns a little farther.

"Don't!" Q's voice rings out, echoing in the hallway over the clicking of bone on stone.

Domina's head freezes.

"Don't," Q repeats softly. "Not another inch."

She looks straight ahead again, her fingers clenching, her Beretta still held in her right hand.

"Just tell me," Q says. "Tell me what you did."

"Part of Maab's conversion technique." Domina's voice is shaky. "Igraine ordered it. It's not my—"

"Which part?" Q asks.

Din shifts his weight from one leg to the other. "The skeletons are back there, and surely they hear us. We've not much time. Your man is alive, you should—"

"*I asked which part!*" Q screams.

Din's shoulders hunch as if weighed down by Q's anger, and I can see Domina shaking.

"What," Q says between clenched teeth, "have you done," his words have a force to them, an inevitability which terrifies me, "to my friend?"

"Look. I know about the agreement with Ares. I know we're not supposed to use conversion techniques on infidels, but we didn't know," Domina begins, and she then pauses, taking a breath. "We didn't know he was—"

In all my life, I have never seen an infidel lose their temper. Q snarls, throwing his gun aside and leaping toward her. She turns, bringing her Beretta to bear, but Q doesn't give a shit. He grabs her by the throat as the gun discharges into his body armor, and slams her against the wall. I expect him to double over from the power of the bullet, but oddly, that doesn't happen.

Din has dropped his gun and is reaching for Q, but the infidel's kick knocks him away. Q raises his right fist over his head while his left hand leaves creases in Domina's throat.

"No!" I shout through my pain. "Q, don't hurt her."

"Look at me!" Q yells at Domina, ignoring my plea, his voice echoing loudly amidst the enclaves. "Look at me you fucking bitch! Look at me or I'll rip your throat out."

Din has his hands in the air.

"Stay cool, Q." Cid's voice washes over us. "Stay cool. He threw his gun down. The truce holds, okay? The truce holds."

But my friend is not moved by her words. Sweat drips off his brow, his fist is shaking with his fury. "There are demons." Q's voice cracks. "They're trying to kill us. All of us. They want us to suffer. And you're doing *that* to people? Why?" He seems truly exasperated. "What in the fuck is wrong with you? Why?"

"Cid," Neb's German accented voice comes from behind Q. "I'm not going to be able to hold them for much longer."

There must be some side passages my friends are using to get around, because I remember his voice coming from the other direction.

"Let her go, Q." El Cid orders. "You heard Neb, we

have to leave."

But Q doesn't respond to Cid at all. "Why?"

Domina struggles for breath, her slender pale hands uselessly gripping Q's arm. "He deserves it," she says, forcing her words out despite his stranglehold on her throat. "All men deserve it. You deserve it. Cris *definitely* deserves it."

Q's fist slams so hard into her face that I'm almost sure he's killed her. The echo of the smack and of the resulting crack of her skull on the stone reverberates down the corridor. She'd have dropped but for his hand around her throat. His punches continue, hooks driven forward by his twisting shoulder, lightning fast, snaking in and out as her head beats out a rhythm on the stone wall.

Din leaps with a shout and grabs Q from behind. My friend lowers his weight, stepping out with one foot, absorbing his attacker's momentum. Din has locked his hands around the nimble Q and is trying to drive him into the wall.

Domina drops like a ragdoll, her unconscious head lolling to one side at an awkward angle, her hair spilling over her shoulder.

Q twists about in the man's grip, his right leg kicking out, wheeling around in the air as Q's graceful muscles force his torso downward. That leg wraps around Din as Q cartwheels over the stone. Din's body, a slave to Q's momentum, rises and then falls. They land, a mass of Carrion man and infidel, upon the stones as Nebuchadnezzar appears out of the haze, skeletons clicking at his back.

I hear Cid shouting, but I can't tell what she's saying.

Domina twitches.

Q has Din beneath him, a knee planted firmly on the Carrion man's belly. Din has his hands raised over his head, trying to protect himself, but Q's blows land repeatedly against the man's ribs. Chainmail chinks violently under the blows, but I'd be surprised if it was offering Din any protection.

"Cris!" Cid shouts.

Oh, she's talking to me.

"Cris, my baby, my love. Sweetheart!"

What nice things she is saying.

"Cris! You have to come to me. You *have* to."

I look back. Domina is not dead. She's alive, and Cid's struggling to get the woman up in her arms. Domina doesn't know what's going on, so she's trying to fight.

"You have to!" Cid begs me.

Maybe.

Nebuchadnezzar kicks back a skeleton, and then another. He bumps into Q on accident, but the infidel doesn't notice except to shift ever so slightly, maintaining his perfect balance. I hear ribs cracking under his next barrage.

Din shouts and lowers his arms to protect his torso, and Q starts in at his head. Bony fingers grab at Q's shoulder, but Neb smacks them away. Cid is there, grabbing at Q and shouting at me, but again, I can't tell what she's saying. Blood whips up into the air from Q's knuckles, sparkling in the light as their droplets paint the dead.

One of the skeletons is bending down by where Cid has abandoned Domina.

That can't happen.

I try to crawl to her.

"No, Cris!" Cid yells. "Away. You have to crawl away."

She grabs Q under the arms, trying to drag him off Din.

Neb is franticly swinging about himself with the butt of a rifle. He looks at me, at where I'm headed. He moves across the corridor and kicks the dead thing which hovers over Domina. Her pale flesh seems unblemished, but she's not moving.

I begin to cry.

"Q!" Cid bends her knees and tries to lift him up. "We've got to go."

Q shucks her off and lands another pair of blows upon Din before skeletal hands reach out and replace Cid's. He's only too glad to share his anger with them. Q is on his feet in moments, his fists snaking out in repetitive combinations like little bits of lightning. His enemies melt away.

"Get him!" Q yells to Neb.

The Nazi grabs me, struggling to help me to my feet, but I can't stand.

"He needs you, Q!" Cid shouts. "Cris needs you."

Q's head whips around, and he sees me, a limp thing in Nebuchadnezzar's arms. In this moment, surely he'll notice I'm not worth his effort. But then he's here, picking me up in his wiry arms with a tenderness that Fellman could never match.

I cry as Q carries me away.

I regain consciousness. They've stopped near the Erebus to tend to my wounds.

And sometimes, I feel . . .

Nebuchadnezzar watches the entrance silently. "He's awake," the necromancer says without turning around. "That's Cris' hellsong."

El Cid is stitching my split rear end faster than I thought possible. The tiny needle in her hand threads through the wound. I have not known pain like this. In, out. In, out. In, out.

Q is wrapping my ankle with similar speed. "Where's Aiden? Was he captured too? Did he fall near you?"

Infidels don't cry.

My world is spinning.

Myla's song becomes a shriek, a shrill banshee howl with the same resonance as the cry of the Furies, echoing like a lost soul in the dark winds of the Erebus. I feel Myla's rage, her anguish, her unspeakable denial tearing down the back of my neck and spine.

But it's not her who's really screaming. The hellsong belies my own sorrow.

El Cid stops for a moment, her needle paused in my flesh, her mouth slightly open. Q's head bows, his eyes closing. Even Nebuchadnezzar has turned toward me.

Cid finishes tying off my stitches, and then holds me in her arms. "Oh, Cris."

Her tears drop onto my neck and run into the collar of my torn shirt.

Infidels do cry.

"Neb," Cid says. "I'm out of gauze, do you have any?"

Q takes up the watch as the Nazi dips into his pack. He produces a roll of gauze.

I'm bewildered. "How?" I ask. "How were you all here to save me?"

"We should have left," Cid says. "You know Jessica, Mason, Eagan and Jenner are waiting for us, and we're long overdue. We tracked Keith's men up to the Catacombs, but the trail was dead. At that point, it was our duty to give up on you.

"But Q wouldn't let us leave. He said that somehow he'd find a sign. We'd been searching the catacombs systematically since we lost your trail, until we heard your captors bedding down for the night."

Neb hands over the gauze. Cid finishes her work quickly.

"Help him get his pants on," she orders the Nazi, "Q, you're on watch. I'll scout out the entryway to the sanctuary."

Q melts into the shadows outside our chamber as Cid disappears into the wilds. I'm alone with Neb.

He kneels at my feet, picking up my pants. The flashing light of the Erebus helps him determine which way is front. He lifts one of my feet and slides it into a pant leg, then repeats the process more carefully on the other.

It only hurts a little.

I look up at his haughty features, at his well-defined cheek bones and light eyes.

He meets my gaze.

"She lied to you, you know," Neb says.

"No," I say. "Cid doesn't lie."

He nods. "Not directly, no. She did say we had to abandon you, and Q did demand we stay." He pauses, helping bunch up the legs of my pants so he can get my left foot through. "But she didn't argue back."

Myla's wail dies away, and all I can hear is the buffeting of the Erebus—then, as I close my eyes, even that goes quiet.

This is what I feared, that after escaping, I'd

discover I had no reason left to live.

"I want to die," I say softly, more to Hell, or to the Erebus, than to Neb.

He shakes his head. "Oh, no. You don't get to die." The words are eerily reminiscent what Keith said when he'd captured me. "And even if you do, I'll just sprinkle a little dust on you, and you'll be right back up on your feet."

The Erebus is but a whisper.

"I saw an Angel, Neb."

He looks at me, blue eyes curious. "You did?"

"That means there's a heaven."

His head tilts upward, as if to stare at that far off realm. "Not for us, Cris. Not for us."

Want to be notified when sequels are released? Register as a Citizen at hellsongseries.com

Need to look up a term?
Check out the Gehennic Encyclopedia as a free download on Kindle or view at our website: hellsongseries.com/encyclopedia

Sisyphean
Publishing

Hellsong Series

What is it like to be damned?

Arturus knows.

Born in Hell, Arturus has never had the chance to meet his creator or seek redemption; but that doesn't mean he has no destiny. He lives near the village of Harpsborough, whose people have torn a moment of peace from the unwilling claws of damnation—and damnation wants it back.

Future omens are poor. Infidels roam the wilds, devils are amassing, and the very stones of Hell themselves have begun to break apart. But even while they fight damnation, Arturus and the hunters of Harpsborough find themselves facing off against traitors from amongst their own ranks and a people they thought they'd left far behind.

Look for *Even Hell Has Knights* and continue exploring the Hellsong Universe!

Hellsong Series

Like a character? Want to follow them through the Hellsong universe?

Cris returns in *Convalescence*.

Cris appears in *Even Hell Has Knights* and *March till Death*.

El Cid, Q and Aiden appear in *Knight of Gehenna* and *March till Death*

A Note from Sipub

Did you enjoy this book? If you did, please keep in mind that we are a small press. Sisyphean Publishing does not have the marketing dollars to match a "big five" or mainstream publisher. We rely on you, our reader, to spread the good word about our amazing tales.

So if you would, take a moment to leave a review at your relevant point of sale, share your thoughts about this novel with a friend, and/or make the appropriate sacrifice/propitiation/prayer to your deity of choice (except for *Kurtulmak*, that would just be awkward) on our behalf!

Sincerely,

Michael Cannon
Director of Distribution
Sisyphean Publishing

Shaun McCoy lives in South Carolina. He is an accomplished Pianist, Cage Fighter, Chess Player and Writer. You can check out his fan page at www.facebook.com/shaunomccoy